Tales of the Were

Lone Wolf

BIANCA D'ARC

Copyright © 2017 Bianca D'Arc
All rights reserved.
ISBN: 1548564052
ISBN-13: 978-1548564056

DEDICATION

This is dedicated to all the lone wolves out there. The ones who march to the beat of their own drum and keep on keepin' on.

I'd also like to offer special thanks to my friend, Peggy, for her insights and to my editor, Jess, for being so accommodating on this particular project, where time ran short to get everything done that we needed to get done. My heartfelt thanks to two great friends and helpers.

And, as always, to my family, who stand by me and encourage me as I keep on livin' the dream. Or, at least, *try* to do so.

PROLOGUE

New York City

"Don't fuck with me, old man." Josh's voice was a deep growl in the dark shadows of the city night.

He didn't like cities for just this reason. Too much noise. Too much concrete. And too many damned Others in too close proximity. It was impossible not to run into them from time to time, when he'd much rather avoid all contact with those of his kind—or close to his kind, at least.

"You don't want to piss off the East Side Alpha, loner scum," one of the werewolves who formed a half-circle around their leader scoffed.

"Watch it, shorty," Josh shot back. "I have no beef with your Alpha. I'm just passing through, minding my own business. I'd appreciate being left alone to attend to it."

"All strays entering our territory are supposed to ask permission of the Alpha. Any mongrel knows that," spat another of the support staff while the leader just watched, his cool eyes evaluating. He was a cagey one.

"How the fuck was I supposed to know there was a Pack infestation in this part of the city? As you already pointed out, I'm a loner. I don't have a Pack or any other affiliations. I walk my path alone. By choice." Josh was getting really annoyed. He didn't owe these pricks an explanation.

"Infestation?" One of the lieutenants growled and surged forward, but the Alpha's hand shot out to hold him back.

"Perhaps you don't know the proper etiquette," the Alpha spoke at last, his words measured and his gaze shrewd. "But seeing as how we've now crossed paths, why don't you give me some reassurance that you aren't here to try to upset my Pack or any Others I'm allied with? This is my territory,

2

and I protect it. Even a loner can understand that, surely?"

Hmm. A thoughtful Alpha. Josh supposed this guy hadn't risen to such a position in this kind of densely populated area without good reason. Josh could respect that, even though the older man currently stood in his way.

"All right, I'll give you that," Josh said, nodding. He gave the appearance of relaxing marginally but was still ready for anything. "I'm here looking for a guy named Duncan. Supposed to be of the magic persuasion. I heard he was up this way, and I've come to find him."

"And what will you do if you locate him? What do you want him for?"

"I need to talk to him." It irked Josh to have to give this dude any more information than strictly necessary. What Josh was doing in New York was his own damned business.

"Talk? You sure that's all? I won't sanction unnecessary violence on my patch." The Alpha knew something. The narrowing of his eyes gave him away.

"Why? You know the guy?"

Josh shifted his weight, trying to appear casual, yet strong. It wasn't a hard pose for someone of his height and stature, even when faced with a werewolf Alpha who was only a couple of inches shorter.

"I might." The wolf cracked a smile. "If he's the one you seek, he needs no protection from me. *You* might, though."

Josh bristled, and his fingers flared, shooting sparks from the tips that dissipated near his feet.

Damn. He really had to get this shit under control.

The lesser werewolves backed away. Only the Alpha stood firm, facing Josh, his expression unreadable. Finally, he spoke.

"What the fuck are you?"

"I wish to hell I knew."

*

Josh hoped to hell that the werewolf Alpha hadn't given him a bum steer. The guy had seemed nice enough once they finally got down to it, but Josh didn't really *know* the man. The Alpha might've sent him to an enemy's door, just for shits and giggles, for all Josh knew.

There was definitely some strange mojo around the house. Expensive. Old. It had an air of blood about it that Josh couldn't quite place. And deeply ingrained protective magic.

It was an old brownstone in the heart of Manhattan. Pricey address. Very upper crust. And the very stone it was made from was steeped in magic. It pulsated in repetitive waves from the place, but it didn't feel malevolent. It was just sort of sitting there…watching. Waiting.

Squaring his shoulders, he mounted the steps, sending up a quick prayer that he wasn't about to let loose the hounds of hell. He reached gingerly for the shiny gold knocker on the door, and when sparks didn't leap out to burn him, he touched his fingers to the cool metal. He tested it for a moment before grasping it to give three firm knocks.

So far, so good. The magic of the house remained at rest, like a sentry eyeing the intruder, waiting for Josh to put a toe wrong before lashing out. He supposed that was a good response. If the magic surrounding the house was evil, it probably would have gone for him already. That seemed to be the response of every creature of ill intent that had crossed his path in recent weeks.

The magic that had suddenly come alive

under Josh's skin was apparently all too tempting for those who wanted it for themselves. Or to serve their evil masters. Neither of which Josh was prepared to allow.

The battles had been bloody and fast. The magic had risen in him, but it was untrained and still unfocused. He'd relied on his fighting skills while the magic did just enough to allow him to get close to his enemies and rip them apart.

He'd left a trail of bodies from the Badlands to the steps of this elegant townhouse, but it couldn't be helped. It had become all too clear that Josh needed help harnessing the power that had inexplicably risen in him, and that quest had led him here, looking for a guy named Duncan.

Was he mage? Josh wasn't sure. But the wise woman who had set him on this path had steadfastly believed that only Duncan— or one like him—could help Josh now. She'd refused to tell Josh the nature of the being he sought, but she'd said that this Duncan fellow was the most likely to be able to help him.

Josh had thanked the old lady and gone on his way before his enemies had found him again. The last thing he'd wanted to do was bring trouble down on the wise woman's doorstep. She'd been kind to him at a time when he'd needed it most, and he wouldn't forget that. If he ever got control of what he'd become, he'd pay her back in some way. He didn't know how, but he'd do it, even if it took the rest of his days.

However long or short that may yet prove to be.

The door opened suddenly, and Josh studied the man across the portal. He was tall. About Josh's height. Powerfully built. A warrior, then. He wasn't a shifter, but he smelled strongly of magic, and the odor of the house…

"Vampire?" Josh was appalled. He'd never had anything to do with bloodletters, and he didn't want to start now.

"Not me. The house belongs to a friend who is of that persuasion," the man said, his voice low and almost…musical. It was an odd thought to have, but it fit. Somehow. "Who are you?"

"My name is Josh. A wise woman sent me to look for a man named Duncan. Is that you?" Josh had come too far to prevaricate now.

The other man's eyes narrowed as if he was considering his reply. "Before I answer your question, tell me...why do you seek Duncan le Fey?"

"Wait a minute, did you say *fey*?" Josh shook his head and looked down at his feet for a moment.

It just figured. He was getting messed up with shit he had no desire to know about. He was a shifter. A werewolf. He'd been hoping the guy he sought was some kind of shifter too. Or, at worst, maybe a mage. But a fucking fey?

Josh hadn't really even considered that the myths about fey might be real, after all, but this guy's words seemed to indicate that they were. Fuck. Why in the world would the wise woman send Josh after a fucking fairy?

"It's not contagious, I assure you." The guy sounded pissed as Josh refocused on the man in the doorway.

"Sorry. I just..." How could he tell the guy he had no desire to meet a fey? He couldn't. Because the shitty truth of it was, he'd probably been sent halfway across the country looking for a fey, though he hadn't realized it at the time. "It just took me by surprise. I had no idea."

"Clearly." Frost came off the guy's words. Yeah, Josh had insulted him. Well, that wasn't anything new. Josh wasn't exactly housebroken when it came to polite society, and judging by this fancy brownstone and the impeccably tailored clothes the man in the doorway was wearing, these folks flossed with gold threads. "My question remains. Why do you seek Duncan, who is fey, apparently much to your surprise and dislike?"

Josh felt the power building again, like it had when he'd been confronted by the local Alpha and his lieutenants. Shit. This kept happening, and he had no idea how to control it. That was just one of the things he needed help with, and it certainly seemed—like it or not—that his quest had led him here, to this swanky house in an upscale part of town.

"This is why." Josh held up his hands, watching the tiny lightning bolts of magical energy gather on his fingertips and then dart toward the sky, where he pointed them. Sky or ground seemed the safest places to let the magic go, but nobody had given him any instruction. He was just following his instincts.

When the charge dissipated, Josh looked back at the man in the doorway. He seemed unimpressed, but he did have a little spark of interest in his eyes, if Josh wasn't mistaken. Was it acquisitive interest? If so, the dude could just stop right there.

"Look. If you want my power, I'll tell you right now, you're not getting it. I've been besieged by evil shitheads ever since this magic ignited a few weeks ago, and not one has bested me yet. All I'm looking for is someone who can tell me what the fuck is going on and help me figure out how to fix it. I was told this Duncan guy could do that. If not, I'm sorry to have wasted your time."

The man bowed his head slightly. "As you surmise, I am Duncan le Fey. And I recognize the flavor of your power. I'm intrigued that you don't seem to know what you are."

"I'm a werewolf," Josh answered immediately, though it had become pretty clear to him over the past few weeks that he was a bit more than that. He wasn't sure why or how, but there was definitely something inside him that set him apart from the other wolves he'd known. Though, as a loner, he didn't really know all that many.

Duncan nodded. "And yet, you're more than a simple wolf." He seemed to come to a decision. "Will you come in so we can discuss this further in more privacy? The house's wards are top notch, but it's still not wise to discuss such matters on the doorstep."

"It smells of vampire in there," Josh said plainly.

"Yes," Duncan answered just as honestly. "My friend, Dante d'Angleterre owns the house, but he is newly mated and currently on his honeymoon. I am house sitting, as it were. Dante is a bloodletter. I am fey."

Duncan could almost see the thought process happening behind his visitor's eyes. Finally, the man shrugged and muttered, "What the hell? I've come this far."

The moment he came to a decision and stepped forward, Duncan moved back so the other man could enter. Duncan studied him as he passed. Werewolf, yes…but even more highly magical than others of his kind. The paradox he presented, just by his existence, was intriguing.

Duncan had met many beings in his long life, but never one with such uncontained power. Familiar power, yet...different. Untrained and with a lethal edge that probably came from his shifter nature.

"The parlor is just through that archway on your left," Duncan directed.

The werewolf didn't hesitate, just stalked into the room and prowled around it for a bit before settling in the only chair with a view of both the front window and the archway. Interesting.

Duncan entered more slowly, selecting his own seat with care. He wanted to be able to keep an eye on both his visitor and the window—in case the man had brought friends or been followed. Duncan waited to see what the werewolf would do next. He didn't have long to wait.

"My name is Joshua McCann. I'm a loner and have been living rough, but not wild, in the Badlands of North Dakota for the past few years. I was doing fine, minding my own business, when out of nowhere, my inner magic has just gone crazy. Suddenly, I had all sorts of people hunting me, confronting me, trying to trap me and steal my power. I've been fighting them off for the past few months. Killed most of them because they didn't give me any choice. It's driving my wolf crazy and making my human side a little nuts, too, with all the moving and running and watching my trail."

Duncan nodded slowly. It was clear his visitor was more than agitated. By what he described, he was being hounded—for lack of a better word, though he doubted the werewolf would appreciate the pun—by those who would steal his power. It was an all-too-familiar story, unfortunately, but this Joshua's flavor of magic put a unique twist on the tired old tale.

"Those who are unscrupulous often seek to steal magic as a shortcut to their own glory. And they often die for it, which I can't fault you for, Mr. McCann." Duncan shrugged. Those mages had brought their fate on themselves when their hearts had turned to evil.

The werewolf stilled for a moment, as if responding to Duncan's deliberately calm demeanor. The last thing Duncan wanted to do was incite the already excitable werewolf. What he needed was to take things down a notch.

The visitor nodded. "Call me Josh."

Good, he was responding, calming even as Duncan watched. Now, maybe, they could get somewhere in discovering what exactly was going on.

"You indicated that the level of magical power was new to you," Duncan began. "Was there some triggering event? Some definitive moment when the magic first manifested?"

"Well, I've always had what I assume was the normal amount of magical awareness for any werewolf. At least according to my mother. She's really the only other werewolf I know well. There was a bear shifter shaman near where we lived that I knew pretty well too, and I always knew he had way more power than either me or Mom."

"Bears are among the most magical of shifters. Did this shaman ever notice anything out of the ordinary with you or your wolf?"

"Not that I know of." Josh shook his head. "There was something... I should explain. I've been roaming alone for a while. I got a job and saved up some money to buy Mom a little place on the outskirts of the nearest large town so she would have some support while I went off to see the world. I didn't want to leave her all alone in the middle of nowhere while I did my own thing."

Duncan nodded. Josh was a conscientious son, which spoke well for his nature and heart.

"Mom seemed happy. She was making new friends among her human neighbors and her place backs onto wilderness, so she can go wolf anytime she wants with little chance of being discovered. I left her there to so I could experience a bit of the world on my own. I was doing okay until one night I came across something I shouldn't have. There was a car crash on the side of a deserted highway in South Dakota. I was I wolf form, but I moved closer to see if I could offer assistance. I smelled a lot of blood and at least seven different human scents. There was also the odor of magic, but it wasn't something I really recognized at that time. It took a while for me to become familiar with the particular reek of blood magic."

Duncan got a sinking feeling in the pit of his stomach. Blood magic was among the most foul...and evil.

"There had been a man in the car that went down an embankment. Another car had crashed into him and was still at the side of the road, with damage, but drivable. Another car had stopped behind that one and was clean. Six people surrounded the bleeding man, who had crawled out of the wreck of his car, and they were chanting. One bent down and dipped his fingers in the blood of the injured man and in my vision, a red flare of magical energy surrounded the circle they'd formed around the bleeding man."

Josh's face reflected the horror he'd probably felt at seeing such things. By his reactions, Duncan was getting a clearer image of what Josh was all about. This was no ordinary werewolf that had come to call. No, Joshua McCann was something altogether different.

"I understood what they were doing, though I'd never seen or heard of anything like that before. Those six had run this guy off the road deliberately and were trying to steal his magic. I realized the bleeding man must've been a mage—as were the six jokers around him. Something inside me just sort of snapped seeing what they were doing to someone who was completely helpless and badly injured. My wolf didn't like the flavor of their magic and I guess…I kind of went a little crazy. I…attacked them."

Josh swallowed visibly, seeming to be lost in the memory.

"You did the right thing," Duncan said quietly, jolting Josh out of the memory and back to the present. "I have no doubt from what you describe that you assessed the situation correctly. I am surprised though, that you were able to survive six mages in wolf form when your magic is untrained. Tell me how the battle went," Duncan invited.

"I pounced on the one with blood on his hands first. I took him from behind, following him down to the ground. I went for his throat and got him before the others seemed to realize what was happening. A quick kill."

"And a justified one, in case you were wondering," Duncan added. "Anyone who deals in the blood of innocents is irredeemable in my book."

Josh tilted his head. "Good to know." He went on to describe the rest of the battle— how the enemies tried to throw magic at him, but they were disorganized by the loss of their leader and then one by one, they were either taken down or ran away. "Two mages ran," Josh concluded. "But they came after me a week or two later and I killed them then. The other four died on the spot. The first, I took out wolf style, like I said, but then something happened. Something sort of exploded inside me and there was this blinding white light." His expression was grim. "I didn't know what was going on, but when I looked around after the flash, the remaining three who had been battering me with magical bolts and fireballs were all on the ground, dead."

"What of the man they'd been attacking?" Duncan asked. The answer to that question would reveal quite a bit.

"He was still breathing," Josh confirmed. "I shifted to human form and carried him up to the damaged car the two runners had left behind. It was okay to drive, just smashed up a bit on the front end. I took the man to a clinic and left him there after I made sure someone found him and took him inside for treatment. Then I went wolf again and took off."

What Josh had just described must've been a very rude awakening of a power that had lain dormant all of Josh's life. It had taken enormous strain of the magical kind to rouse his innate power, but when it had happened, it had done the right thing—destroying evil and protecting the innocent. Duncan could work with that.

In fact, he would *encourage* that in any being, but particularly a werewolf hybrid of such power that a single blast of his magic could take out three evil mages at once. They'd need people with such abilities if the Destroyer should return to this realm, as Duncan very much feared was about to happen.

"You said the other two hunted you after that," Duncan prompted Josh to continue with his tale.

"Yeah," Josh rubbed a weary hand through his shaggy hair. "Them and all their evil little buddies. It's been battle after battle ever since. I couldn't go back to visit Mom. I didn't want to bring violence to her door, though I've been able to call her now and again. I haven't told her what's been happening. I didn't want to worry her."

"What of your sire? Is he also a werewolf?" Duncan asked, having to stop himself from leaning forward in anticipation of the answer.

"Never met him. He left before I was

born and Mom won't talk about him. I don't ask because I know it hurts her. He was human I've always assumed he didn't feel the mating bond the same way Mom did."

It was significant to Duncan that the young man didn't seem to know or care about his sire's origins. A spell perhaps? Or hurt feelings? Perhaps he had cultivated a disinterest to protect his mother in some way. From what Duncan knew of shifters, if one mate disappeared, the other was likely to suffer greatly, perhaps even die of the heartbreak. That Josh's mother had survived to raise him spoke well for her, and the warmth in Josh's voice when he talked about his mother impressed Duncan greatly. Family was important, even to fey, though he knew it was the vital center of shifter existence.

"So, what led you to my door, Josh?" Duncan asked in that same gentle tone. He'd already learned more about the man than the young werewolf realized, but he needed to know more.

Josh sat back, more at ease with the turn of the conversation. "A wise woman in Indiana sent me in this direction, to find you specifically. She said you might be able to help me."

"A wise woman, indeed." Duncan sat back in his chair and regarded the younger man. He weighed the available options and came to a quick decision. "I'm afraid that I'm going to have to send you on to another wise woman. You need some time away from the hunt to regroup and rebuild your energies. You also need a bit of peace and quiet in which to learn to control your newfound magic."

"I do?" Josh looked as if he wanted to agree, but also like he wanted to rip something apart in frustration. Then, he subsided. "Yeah, I do." He ran one hand through his shaggy hair. "But I'm no fit company for a delicate female right now."

"She is female, and delicate by some standards, but she is more powerful than you might expect, and she's the perfect person to give you a chance at healing before you tackle those who would continue to harass you." Duncan leaned forward, watching Josh intently. "The first thing you need to know is that the power coursing through your veins right now is of the fey realm. Somehow, a channel has opened up between you and your lost heritage. I'm not sure how or why, but, my friend, I am in no doubt as to your nature. You're at least part fey."

Josh looked stunned. "No fucking way."

Duncan only smiled.

CHAPTER ONE

Lancaster County, Pennsylvania

Deena Lovett patted her horse, Buccaneer, on the nose as she left the barn. She didn't strictly need to have a horse, but she figured it was one of the perks of living out here in the middle of Pennsylvania Amish country. She could take in all the strays she wanted, and nobody could complain. In fact, her neighbors often shook their heads at the odd assortment of critters she'd collected around her.

There was Samson, the retired plow horse, and Maisy, the aging cow. Both had come to her as payment for services rendered, though she didn't usually request

23

payment of any kind. She operated on a barter system that kept her in fresh produce, eggs and dairy, while allowing her to help neighbors with her healing skills.

Every once in a while, though, when she visited a farm where one of her patients lived, she felt the pull of an animal spirit. Usually, it was an animal that wanted a peaceful life after years of service to an ungrateful owner. While most farmers cherished their animals, there were a few— thankfully precious few—who saw their stock only as commodities.

Samson and Maisy would have been sold to a slaughterhouse if Deena hadn't asked for them in payment, and the animals knew it. Or sensed it. Deena wasn't clear on just how much they comprehended, but they certainly understood emotion. They knew when unkind thoughts were directed at them.

Buccaneer had come to her in a similar way, but he'd just been a foal at the time. A foal born with a bad leg that his owner could not afford to fix. Deena had taken one look at the limping foal and fallen in love. She'd also known that, with time and all her skill, she would be able to help the little fella.

And so, she had. Buccaneer had grown into a fine specimen, and in recent years, he'd become sought after as a stud by some of the more adventurous farmers. So far, all of his foals had been born without any problems, proving that the leg issue hadn't been genetic, but rather an accident of the way he'd come into this world.

Either way, Deena loved him, and she sensed a similar feeling from him. Horses were amazingly intelligent, if a bit high strung, and she enjoyed them tremendously. As she walked into the stable yard, she was greeted by two more of her residents. They were newcomers, but they were proving to be the comic relief.

Pedro and Maria were alpacas. They had fluffy white and curly light brown fur, respectively. They'd both developed a bad infection that had almost taken their lives, along with the rest of their herd, but the farmer had finally called her after the local veterinarian had given up. Deena had cured the herd, and the farmer had given her the pair of elder fluff-butts in thanks.

Deena was currently learning how to shear the alpacas, and then, she might be able to use their super-soft wool to knit

things. It got cold enough in the winter—
and boring enough, at times—to make her
interested in the idea of filling some of her
hours knitting by the fire. Plus, alpaca wool
was way better than sheep's wool. No lanolin
to contend with, and it wasn't itchy. That
was a big advantage. And if Deena couldn't
use it herself, there was always a market for
the stuff, so she could sell it and keep Pedro
and Maria in style.

They followed her around the barnyard a
lot of the time, two big, fluffy shadows.
Today, though, after greeting her, they
retreated into the barn's open door. That
was unlike them, so Deena opened her
senses, wondering what was going on. Sure
enough, she felt the change in the magic
surrounding her land. Someone was nearing
her outermost ward.

Intrigued, Deena walked toward the
house, keeping an eye toward the long drive
that led in from the road. Her wards were set
all around the boundaries of her property.
She would know the moment the owner of
the strange magic crossed onto her land.

Josh wasn't altogether sure about this.
Duncan had snuck him out of Manhattan in

the dead of night, using his considerable fey magic to foul their trail. The trip from New York to the farmland of Pennsylvania hadn't been too long. Just over three hours by car, and they were looking at rolling fields and cow pastures.

Duncan had dropped Josh literally at the side of the road with a letter in his hand. He'd pointed the way up a long, dusty gravel drive and then sped off. Josh knew that Duncan was going onward to throw any possible tails off his track, but it still felt a lot like being abandoned by the only person who had even half a clue about Josh's current problem.

And now, here he was, a stranger in a very strange land. Josh had lived rough, but he'd never lived on what looked like a working farm, with the strangest amalgamation of animals he'd ever seen together in one place. He swore he'd even seen two alpacas before they ran away in fright from his inner wolf.

There didn't seem to be any rhyme or reason to the collection of animals. Most looked past their prime. As if this was some kind of weird retirement home for old creatures who'd been put out to pasture.

Only these animals looked well cared for. Not as if they'd been forgotten when the useful portion of their lives had passed.

They had glossy coats and what he judged to be happy expressions, though they all eyed him with suspicion. At least the ones that had stuck around to watch him walk up the gravel drive. The more timid had already fled into the barn, or maybe behind it, putting space between themselves and the predator that lived in Josh's soul.

Josh felt a little thrill of magic sparking off his own when he crossed over some invisible barrier. He paused and shook his head.

"What the hell was that?" he said aloud, to himself.

"That was my ward. You are now trespassing on my land." The soft voice came from behind him. Josh spun, but no one was there. He turned back, his head on a swivel, wondering if he'd imagined the feminine tones.

And then, there she was. Standing just in front of the porch of the sprawling farmhouse, looking dainty and demure in her denim skirt and worn baseball jersey. She had mud-covered boots on her feet and heavy work gloves in one hand, as if she'd just taken them off.

"Are you the priestess?" Josh asked, unwilling to show how uncomfortable he was with the fact that she'd managed to sneak up on him.

Her head tilted as if she was considering his words, then she nodded. Just once. "Who are you?"

"My name is Joshua McCann. I have a letter here from a mutual friend named Duncan. He wanted me to give it to you. I think he explained a bit about me in there, though I haven't read it myself." Josh held up the sealed envelope in one hand as she walked toward him.

He tried to move, but discovered his feet were glued in place somehow. He was restrained by magical means, and he suddenly realized just how powerful this small woman might be. He'd never had too much to do with priestesses—at least until recently—but all shifters who followed the Light respected them and their reputed power. He was intrigued to learn the reputation wasn't an exaggeration. This woman held him in place without much effort, judging by her casual stroll down from the house to meet him.

She stopped just out of arm's reach, darting forward briefly to take the letter out of his hand. She retreated immediately to her safe distance where he couldn't grab her or try anything physical, frozen as he was by her magic.

She opened the letter and spent a moment reading it over, her expression giving nothing away. When she was done, she looked up at him, squinting a little as if giving him some sort of once-over.

"Well, aren't you just a furry ball of surprises?" she finally said.

He wasn't imagining it. She was definitely looking him up and down now. He almost asked if she wanted to check out his teeth while she was at it. He felt like he was being sized up to see if he was worthy to join the other animals in her barn.

"I'm not sure what Duncan said in the letter, but I need help from someone who knows what the hell is going on with my magic all of a sudden. I got sent to Duncan by a wise woman, and now, he's pushed me off onto you." Frustration sounded in his voice, but he didn't care. "If you want to pass the buck on to someone else, then I'll gladly leave, but I'm getting tired of being sent on wild goose chases."

She considered him for a moment. "It must irk your inner wolf to never actually catch the goose, right?" Then, she smiled, just faintly, but it was a friendly smile all the same. "All right. I can see you've had a rough time, and that's kind of my specialty." She gestured around her at all the misfit animals in her care. "I'll try to help you, but we need to set a few ground rules first."

He regarded her steadily. "What are your terms?"

"First, no going wolf in front of my livestock. Some of them have been traumatized enough already and don't need to realize there's a giant predator living among them. If you need to shift, there's a cornfield out back. I'm sure there are vermin trails out there that might satisfy any hunting or tracking need you might feel. Or you could make yourself useful and patrol the borders of my land. I have wards—as you've already experienced—but extra vigilance is never wasted. You just have to be stealthy about it and not be seen by my neighbors. They're okay with dogs, but massive wolves might stir them into a tizzy." The corners of her mouth tilted up a bit in humor, and he found himself watching her mouth more than he probably should.

"I can agree to that," he told her, deliberately looking away so he wouldn't stare at her lips too long. "What else?"

"I mentioned the neighbors. They're mostly Amish, which means they won't be thrilled at me—a single woman—having a single man living under my roof. We'll have to pretend to be related if anyone comes around. I'm not sure if they'll believe it, but it's worth a try."

Josh had to stifle a laugh. "Okay, cuz."

She smiled and tilted her head, studying him again. "I'm Deena Lovett, by the way. Where are you from?"

"I grew up in North Dakota, but my mother is from a small Canadian Pack originally."

"Where is she now?" Deena asked, a little frown on her face.

"Still in North Dakota. She's got a little place on the edge of a larger town. She's safe." He decided to share a bit more since this woman seemed genuinely concerned. "I realized I couldn't go home when my magic started attracting all the wrong sorts of attention from all the wrong people. I couldn't bring that kind of danger to her door."

"I'm sorry," she told him, and he believed her. She had a compassionate face. Something he hadn't seen too often living in the wild these past months.

Josh tried to shrug off her words…and his reaction to them. He'd only just met this woman. He didn't understand why she got to him so easily. Maybe it was some kind of priestess mojo. Yet, the wise woman he'd dealt with earlier on his journey hadn't affected him this way. Not at all.

"So. The rules." She took a deep breath as if regrouping. "No magic practice in the house. I have a shielded circle out back in a stand of trees you can use. It's safer, and nobody will bother you there."

"I'll do my best. I should warn you, though, that I get a little out of control at times just lately, and the magic seems to want to ground itself." She was nodding, so he went on. "That's why I've been seeking help. It was never this way before, and it's begun to attract too much interest from bad-intentioned mages."

She gave him another one of her gentle

smiles. "Don't worry. I can help you with that. We'll fix you right up and have you back to your old self—only stronger—in no time."

CHAPTER TWO

Two days later, Josh was out in the back of the house, chopping wood to work off some of his excess energy. Deena had been true to her word, teaching him from within the first few moments of their meeting to ground and center his magic. Once she'd released him from the spell that had frozen him in place, she'd taken him directly to the small circle of stones hidden in a thicket of trees. He'd felt the magical wards, knowing what they were this time, as he passed into the circle.

Deena had taught him the rudiments of shield formation and had left him to practice the skill for about an hour while she'd seen to her daily work in the house and barn.

He'd felt safe within the circle. It felt as if the wards had hidden his wild magic from anyone who might be looking for it. The first hour in that sacred circle had been some of the first peace he'd had in months. And then, she'd returned, and the real work had begun.

He got the feeling she'd cleared her schedule to make time to work with him. He was grateful but wasn't really sure how to express his profound gratitude. He'd started fixing things around the farmstead. There was a rough patch on part of the barn roof he'd replaced yesterday, and today, he was trying to stock up the woodpile he'd found around the back of the house, so she'd be all ready for colder weather.

He'd noted the wood-burning stove in the kitchen and the fireplace in the living room of her home when she'd invited him in for dinner. He'd eaten with her, then spent the night in a guest room on the first floor. It looked like it had been added on to the sprawling farmhouse at some point in the last seventy years or so, sticking out from the side of the house in an asymmetrical way.

Josh had heard her footsteps pattering around above his head. He knew there wasn't an enclosed room above him, but since she was walking around right above him, there probably was some kind of patio space on the flat roof above the addition. Likely, it was a private spot connected to the master suite. Must be nice to stargaze from up there before going to bed.

Imagining her up there in her pajamas— or nothing at all—looking out at the stars made him yearn for things he was better off not thinking about. At least not now. Not until he got his rogue magic under control somehow.

"That's quite the wood pile." Her voice shook Josh out of his reverie. He'd been so lost in thought and memory she'd managed to sneak up on him.

Now, *that* wasn't something that happened to him every day. Maybe she used her magic to assist? If not, he was in big trouble, because inattention at a time like this could easily get him killed and his magic drained by any one of the mages who'd been on his trail the past few months.

Josh tried to be cool as he set the ax head on the ground and leaned casually on the long handle. She walked around to face him, and he followed her progress with his eyes.

She was just as beautiful today, the pale morning sunlight shimmering off her hair, as she had been the moment he first set eyes on her. Just as unattainable. Just as off-limits.

She was a holy woman, and he was a holy terror. A fuck-up of the first order. An angel like her deserved a man who was as upright as she was. Not a lone wolf drifting through life with little aim except to stay alive from day to day and do his best not to let his magic be drained by those with evil intent.

"I figured you could use a stockpile with Winter just around the corner," he told her, trying his best to look and sound nonchalant. She didn't need to know that it was stress and the inner turmoil of his wolf that had him out here chopping wood, sweating and exerting, hoping the physical activity would blunt his antsy mood.

"Oh, it won't go to waste. Thank you. But you don't have to knock yourself out, you know. I suspect you'll be here for a while as we work on your training. You can pace yourself a bit." Her smile was friendly, but he could see a hint of concern in her soft blue eyes.

He didn't like that. He didn't want her to waste her energy worrying about him. He was okay. He *had to be* okay.

"I'm used to working," he replied, hoping she wouldn't probe further. He needed the activity to calm his inner beast, which was still in a bit of turmoil over the changed state of his magic.

The wolf part of him didn't know what to think about the magic that had suddenly surfaced. It was fighting the change—when bad guys weren't trying to kill him—and the inner conflict was really messing with Josh's head. Deena had asked Josh about how his magic had surfaced at dinner the night before, and he'd found himself telling her the story of the car wreck. He'd gone into much more detail about his feelings with her than he'd revealed to Duncan. Somehow Deena had gotten under his skin, but he found he didn't mind it too much. Slowly, he was coming to trust her.

If only his inner wolf would learn to trust the new magic inside him. At present, the only time the wolf worked with the magic was when he was threatened. The survival instinct kicked in at such times, and the dual sides of Josh's nature worked in a beautiful kind of harmony to protect him.

At all other times, the wolf seemed

suspicious of the new magic, and the magic itself bounced around as if unsure where to go or what to do. That had to be a reflection of Josh's uncertainty, of course, since the priestess and those he'd spoken to before her all agreed that the magic was an innate part of Josh that had been repressed in some way until just recently.

Why or how that had occurred wasn't as important as fixing the problem now, while evil was on his trail. Maybe there'd be time later to figure out where it had all gone awry, but at the moment, survival was the first order of business. Josh had to adapt and overcome if he was going to survive.

"The moon will be full tonight," Deena finally said, merely nodding to his earlier statement as he breathed a sigh of relief.

"Yeah," he agreed.

A werewolf always knew the phase of the moon, even if the folklore among humans was wrong about their inability to shapeshift at other times. Josh could turn into his wolf form at any time. The pull was just a little stronger—make that *a lot* stronger—when the moon was riding high and full in the sky.

"I'll be doing a ceremony as the moon rises tonight in the stone circle. You're welcome to join me." She seemed almost shy about her invitation, which made him think she didn't usually invite others to observe her rituals.

"I'd be honored." He nodded his head in respect, holding her gaze. "I haven't been to a full moon rite presided over by a real priestess since I was a child."

There it was. The slightly timid smile he'd hoped to bring to her face. He felt like he'd just won the lottery, odd as it seemed. Why was this small woman so special to him? He'd barely known her for more than the blink of an eye.

"I haven't had a werewolf—or a shifter of any kind, actually—in my ritual circle since I moved here. It'll be a treat for both of us."

He set the ax aside and faced her. "But I'm not fully *were*, am I?"

He'd been waiting for her to tell him what was wrong with his magic for two days, but although she'd been very forthcoming in teaching him how to ground and center, shield and release his new magic, she hadn't really told him anything about her conclusions.

Deena sighed heavily and stepped closer to him, holding his gaze. She wasn't demurring. She wasn't backing down. He liked that about her.

"No, Josh, you're not. Your mother is a werewolf, but I believe your father was something not of this world. Tell me, does she ever speak of him to you?"

A tremor went through him that had nothing to do with an earthquake. It was more like a soul-quake. Something felt by him, and him alone, rocking his world off its axis, and then back on. She probably couldn't tell how her words had affected him, but he felt it down to the depths of his being.

"Mom doesn't talk about him. I do know she loved him until it broke her heart. They were true mates, but one day, he just disappeared, never to be heard from again."

Josh didn't go so far as to curse the absent father he had never met—curses were serious in his world, and he didn't speak them lightly—but he felt the same old anger. The anger at a man he had never met for hurting the one person who loved Josh unconditionally.

Josh loved his mother deeply. He still worried about her, out there on her own. When he'd been small, she'd protected him, but in the past few years, he'd been the one protecting her, and it didn't sit well that he'd had to leave her alone and vulnerable because he was being hunted. Still, there'd been no alternative. To stay near her was to invite those hunting him to target her, as well.

"It's just possible that your father's disappearance wasn't his fault," Deena said slowly, moving a step closer. "The wild magic you're feeling is part of you. A gift from your father's lineage, I believe. He may still be alive, only not in this realm. If he still exists, he's most likely back where he came from, in the fey realm."

Josh wasn't totally surprised by the idea of fey magic, but that she thought it came from his father was a new and startling thought. When Duncan had hinted that Josh might have fey blood, he'd just assumed it had crept in somewhere far back on his mother's side of the family. Josh had honestly never entertained the idea that his father was anything other than human.

"You're saying you think my father is fey." It wasn't a question.

"Fey do pass into our world from time to time, though they do not often stay unless for some greater purpose, like Duncan, who directed you to my door. He is a warrior on the side of good, and he stays here to aid in the battle against evil."

Deena's eyes were getting spooky as she spoke, glowing with an unearthly light. Josh's senses went on alert. His wolf watched, sniffing and suspicious. Something was happening here that he didn't fully understand.

"Deena?"

Deena's lips smiled full and beautifully unabashed. Very unlike the shy smiles she'd given him until now. And those eyes... Those glowing eyes. The spirit looking out of the priestess's eyes wasn't like anything Josh had ever seen before.

"Priestess?" He tried again.

"Yes. She is Our priestess." The presence in Deena's body blinked, and the pure Light of Her dimmed not one bit. If Josh wasn't mistaken, he was addressing one of the aspects of the Goddess, mind-blowing as that might seem. *"We have been watching you, Joshua, for a long time. We have been waiting to see which way you would turn. Now is your time of decision. Do you continue towards the Light? Or do you succumb to the evil that shadows your path?"*

"I will never give in to evil, milady," he felt the need to respond. He felt the truth of his words and the conviction in them ring in his soul. "I serve the Light now, and will always serve the Light."

The spirit in Deena's body tilted Her head in acknowledgment. *"Good. Your words and your strength of spirit are resolute. You will need that in the coming trials."*

Josh didn't like the sound of that.

"Milady, I'm honored beyond words that You have chosen to show Yourself to me. What can I do for You?"

"Much," She said at once. *"Or nothing. It will depend on the outcome of the next weeks. Learn well from Our servant and prepare to use the magic of your forefathers to protect the innocent. We know your sire, Joshua. He is a true and loyal servant of the Light. Will you follow in his footsteps?"*

Josh's father was alive? And he served the Goddess? That was more information than he'd ever had about the man who'd sired him. Josh wasn't sure how to feel about it— or this amazing visitation. To Josh's knowledge, the Goddess didn't speak directly to people very often, and if She did, nobody was talking about it. There was one thing Josh did know for certain, though. He knew he would never give in to evil.

"I have always tried serve the Light in whatever capacity I could," he replied.

Deena's head nodded as if pleased, Her luminous eyes shining bright. *"You have been, and will continue to be, tested by evil, We are sorry to say. What evil does is not in Our control. Neither is how you respond. That is up to your free will. But if you stand strong, We will see you again, Joshua. We have a role in mind for you, if you make it through the trials ahead. Know that We are watching over you, and We will assist where We can, but the hard part will be up to you. You and Our servant, sweet Deena, whom We release to you now."* The Goddess smiled mischievously. *"Better catch her."*

The intense Light blinked out, and Deena's eyes returned to normal for a split second before she wilted, her knees giving way. Josh stepped forward, his wolf lending him preternatural speed so that he caught her before she hit the ground.

Deena had a sense of vertigo, then of falling and being caught in strong arms. Masculine arms. Sexy arms, attached to the most handsome man she'd ever met.

Wait. What?

She tried to touch her head, but her hand wouldn't cooperate. A lethargy kept her whole body compliant in Josh's arms.

Josh. That's who'd caught her. Sexy, magical, lone wolf, Josh.

As her brain started to come back online, she blinked her eyes open to look up at him. His brown gaze was tender and full of concern.

"Are you okay?" he asked, his gruff voice tempered with gentleness. Was this how he'd sound with a lover? And where, exactly, had *that* thought come from?

"What happened?" The two words were about all she was capable of at the moment. Something had drained her, and she was very much afraid she knew what had happened.

"The Goddess..." His words trailed off as if he couldn't quite believe what he'd just seen. She was familiar with that response. Unfortunately.

"Used my body to say hello, did She?" Strength was returning to her more readily as she dealt with the fallout of the Goddess's possession. It had happened often enough that Deena was able to bounce back a little more easily each time.

"That sort of thing happen a lot?" His

lips quirked up in a smile, and she noticed that he hadn't set her back on her feet yet. She wasn't sure she wanted him to, which was somewhat surprising. She'd never warmed so quickly to a man, but Josh was something altogether different in her experience.

"Occasionally. It seems I'm an easy conduit for Her."

CHAPTER THREE

"That's…"

Josh stifled his first instinct to say how totally fucked up that was. He'd been roaming alone for so long, his language had become a bit more than crass. His mama would definitely not approve. He had to remind himself to clean up his filthy mouth around the lady.

"That's pretty amazing," he said instead. "But doesn't that put you at greater risk than most of your kind? I mean, it's a rare being who can commune directly with the Mother of All, right? The bad guys must really hate you for that."

She surprised him with a smile. "Why do you think I live way out here, all on my own?"

She gestured weakly with one hand to the cornfield behind her house and the view that didn't have a single other home in sight. Her home was, indeed, isolated, even though she didn't live too far from civilization. There were towns all around with shopping centers and all the conveniences of modern life if she cared to drive about twenty minutes in any direction.

And there was a key North-South highway only a few miles away. That was the road Duncan had driven them in on. From that major artery, she could go just about anywhere.

Judging by the lack of strength in her hand and arm when she tried to point out the view, Josh realized she wasn't quite ready to be put back on her own feet. He began walking toward the house. There were chairs and a couch in the living room that he could set her down on without causing her any injury. She probably needed to rest after that divine visitation. It sure looked to him that channeling the Goddess took its toll on a body.

"You can put me down," she protested as he walked up the steps on the back porch.

He looked down at her face...so close, he wanted to go that extra few inches and match his lips to hers.

What?

Wait a minute.

Josh had been attracted to the priestess from the moment he'd first seen her, but such a delicate creature was not for him. No. He needed a shifter mate. A female wolf he could howl with and really let loose his inner animal. Deena was far too genteel and fragile for a monster like him.

Right?

Then why was he thinking so hard about kissing her into the next millennium? Why did his heart speed at the thought of learning her taste and touch? Why did his arms tremble, just the tiniest bit, at holding her so close?

This would never do.

"I don't think so," he said, moving toward the back door, which, thankfully, was just enough ajar that he could get his toe in the gap and open it.

He carried her through the kitchen and into the living room, depositing her on the overstuffed couch as gently—and quickly—as he could. Then he backed off, removing himself from temptation. He went to stand near the archway that led back toward the kitchen and escape.

"I'm sorry if I scared you." She sat up, pushing her hair back from her forehead and taking a deep breath as if to refortify herself.

Now wait just a damn minute. He hadn't been scared. How dare she think that about him?

He had to set her straight before he escaped her presence. He couldn't leave her thinking he'd been a scaredy cat.

"I wasn't frightened. Amazed, maybe. Surprised. But not scared. How could anyone be afraid of Her?" He heard the wonder in his own voice. He hadn't meant to reveal so much, but now that he'd let his innermost thoughts out into the light, he didn't regret it.

"Yeah. That's what I always wonder, but more often than not, people get quite a shock when She chooses to reveal Herself. Glad it was a positive experience for you, though." Deena sat more solidly on the couch. She was recovering before his eyes, her spirit more present with each breath, coming back from wherever it had been while the Goddess had used her body.

"Does this happen a lot?" He wanted to escape, but he felt compelled to know more about this strange woman and her incredible gifts.

"Whenever it's important. When She feels the need to get Her message directly to those who need to hear it." She sat up straighter. "Since I've been living out here, She's had a way of directing specific people to my door that She wants to have a chat with. I figure that means the message has to be pretty urgent, for Her to go to such lengths. But it's all good. She put this whole thing in motion. My presence here, in the middle of nowhere, is all according to Her plan. My ability to channel Her words is a dangerous gift. I've been targeted before. I've been chased, hunted, trapped and nearly killed more than once. Living way out here seems to be the best alternative of the choices available."

Josh understood about being hunted. His problems had started more recently than hers, but he had a great deal of compassion for the life she must have lived until now. Being a target sucked. Big time.

Deena tried to get up but swayed a bit too much on her feet. She would have fallen except Josh moved as fast as his inner animal allowed, to catch her once again.

"Sorry," she whispered, looking up at him. The moment seemed to stretch as their gazes met...and held.

This time, Josh ignored the little voice in his head that told him this wasn't a good idea. He lowered his mouth to hers, meeting her soft lips in a gentle kiss.

Why in the world had he thought this *wasn't* a good idea in the first place?

She tasted like heaven and fit perfectly in his arms. He'd noticed that before, the first time he'd had to catch her. She just felt *right*. As if in his arms was where she belonged. Always.

Whoa. Dangerous thought. But it didn't seem to matter. Not as long as his lips were on hers and she was all yielding softness in his arms.

Deena lost all sense of the world around her for those moments when Josh's lips touched hers. It wasn't like the warm nothingness she felt when the Goddess borrowed her body.

No, this time, Deena was fully present, fully involved in the moment, but her focus had narrowed down to just the two of them.

Josh's strong body close to hers, their lips touching, their mouths opening... consuming...combining.

It was heaven. Or, at least, as close as one could come while still on Earth.

She liked the stroke of his tongue and the taste of him. A little wild, a touch exotic. Shifter...and intense magic. She felt his power tingle along her skin, their energies feeling each other out on the magical level while their bodies got to know each other on the earthly plane.

Each connection drew them nearer. She could get drunk on his kisses, though his magical energy nearly singed her senses with its intense, incredible, absolutely stunning power. But it wasn't a power that could hurt her. Quite the contrary. His power seemed to intensify hers, feeding it, helping it grow.

Now wasn't that interesting?

This had never happened to her before. It felt like the fey in her own background was reaching out to caress—or be caressed by— the fey magic in him. There was a hum where their power joined...and meshed. Compatible on a level most beings wouldn't even recognize, much less experience.

Wow. A sizzle of reactive magic made her

pull away, as if a little jolt of benign lightning had just struck the spot between them. She could feel the residual electricity against her exposed skin and smell the faint odor of ozone between them.

"What the hell was that?" Josh murmured, his gaze still half-lidded with pleasure but rapidly growing aware of the hint of danger that had just sparked between them. She could see the predator in his eyes, and for the first time in her life, she was attracted to the wildness in a man's soul.

She'd known her share of shapeshifters, but as much as she loved helping defenseless animals, the predators that shared the shifters' spirits had never done anything for her. Oh, they were handsome enough. All shapeshifters seemed to be blessed with impeccable physiques and chiseled features. But she'd never been tempted to get this close to one of them before.

Maybe it was that Josh was only half-shifter. Then again, the wild wolf in his eyes right now seemed to speak to her on some unconscious level in a way no other shifter predator ever had. Maybe it was just Josh. Maybe he was the key. The reason for the attraction was the man himself...in all his complexity.

"Our magic is compatible on a basic level, but there are differences," she explained, drawing farther away from him once she felt steady on her feet. "There are bound to be sparks when any two magic users get as close as we just were. Physical proximity intensifies the reaction of my magic brushing against yours. Believe me, it could've been a lot worse. In general, we're a lot more compatible than most."

"If that's compatible, I'd hate to experience incompatibility," he said, shaking his head as full awareness returned. She felt a dash of feminine pride that her kiss had been able to muddle his keen shifter senses for even that small space of time.

She had to chuckle at his words. "Explosions are not unheard of," she told him.

"I'd say that was pretty explosive just now," he mused, his mouth turning up at the corners in a bad boy grin that made her insides quiver.

He was just too handsome. Josh was appealing in almost every way. And his magic meshed well with hers. What were the odds?

She tore her gaze away from his and moved around him, heading for the kitchen. She needed a glass of water.

Or maybe she could just dunk her whole head under the open tap. Just for a minute or two. Maybe he wouldn't notice the steam coming off her skin or the flush on her cheeks.

As she filled a glass at the kitchen sink, she glanced out the window, noticing the pony cart just visible along the edge of the cornfield. Little Grace had come to visit with her black and white pony, Mergatroid, clopping along at a jaunty pace.

The pony was small. Not as small as a true miniature horse, but not the size of what most people thought of as a pony. His attitude, though, was as big as any of the much larger carriage horses that shared the family barn.

Deena smiled, watching them approach.

"Company?" Josh's voice came from behind her.

Drat. How was she going to explain his presence to Grace? For it was a certainty that Grace would carry the news back to her mother, and within a day, it would be spread all over the surrounding farms. The Amish were masters of the grapevine, even without telephones.

"Yeah. The youngest daughter from a neighboring farm. She comes around sometimes to visit my animals and learn about healing them. She brings me patients sometimes too. Sweet kid. And her family is a kind one."

"So I get to try out my Cousin Josh from North Dakota disguise?"

She met his gaze, finding amusement sparkling in his eyes.

"It's worth a try," she said, wondering if Grace would accept the story.

Innocent as she was, she wasn't ignorant. She'd probably see the attraction sparking between Deena and her supposed cousin.

"We can be kissin' cousins," Josh whispered near her ear.

When she turned to swat him, he was already halfway across the kitchen, heading toward the guest room she'd given him. Good. Maybe he was going to put on a clean shirt.

"Try not to say anything unless we have to," she called after him. They might get away without too many questions from little Grace this time, but Deena was sure the next time she ran into one of her neighbors, there were going to be a lot of questions to answer. She only hoped she knew what to say when that time came.

CHAPTER FOUR

When Josh stepped outside a few minutes later, he found himself smiling at the scene before him. The little black and white pony basked in Deena's attention while a young girl in Amish dress, who must be Grace, talked in quiet tones, working to unhitch the happy pony from the small cart.

Josh approached cautiously. He didn't want to spook either the animals—for he could scent more than just the pony as he drew closer—or the females.

"Grace, this is my houseguest, Joshua," he heard Deena say.

She hadn't turned, which meant she was becoming as aware of him as he was of her. Interesting.

The girl looked up, surprise on her face. Wide blue eyes met his, and he tried to look as unassuming as possible. He didn't want to be the ogre that went around scaring little girls.

"Josh, this is Grace and her pony, Mergatroid. They live on the next farm over. Grace's father and brothers run a dairy herd, and they've sent me a small patient. Would you give us a hand lifting him out of the cart?"

Josh had scented the calf in the back of the cart and moved around to peer down into the small compartment. Sure enough, there was a little black and white calf with what looked like a broken leg. Josh shook his head. To his admittedly limited knowledge, such an injury wasn't something most people would even try to heal on this kind of animal.

Nevertheless, he scooped the calf into his arms as gently as he could and walked over to the barn, placing the little guy where Deena directed, on a pile of soft straw. The Amish girl trailed behind them, saying nothing.

Deena got right down on the floor with the calf, running her hands over its shaking body. She frowned a few times, but after a thorough examination, she looked up, her gaze skipping from Josh to Grace.

"Can you help him?" Grace asked in a piping voice that fit her small body.

"I think so. But it will take a long time before he can walk properly on this leg. He'll be missing his mama, and his mama will be missing him too," Deena said softly.

"Oh, no," Grace answered. "His mama died in the accident that hurt his leg. My father said if you wanted the calf, you could have him. The injury was beyond him, and he said to leave the calf's fate in the hands of the Almighty."

Deena nodded solemnly. "We are all in the hands of the Divine," she agreed. "I will take in the calf and do my best to help him heal. If it is the Almighty's will, he will live. And you can come visit him anytime you like."

That put a smile on the girl's face. "Oh, thank you, Miss Deena. Thank you for taking him in."

Deena nodded, smiling. "It's all right. Do you want to help me set the bones?" Grace scrambled into the box stall and eagerly knelt at Deena's side. "Josh, would you bring me the red nylon bag from the tack room and a bucket of clean water from the spigot?"

Josh went off to fetch and carry, bemused. He spent the next hour doing whatever Deena asked while she patiently taught Grace about how to set bones. She was a good teacher and a good doctor. She did her best to calm the skittish calf, and it lay docile while she worked on it with the medical kit Josh had fetched.

At one point, Josh looked up to find Mergatroid standing next to him at the entrance of the stall. He looked for all the world as if he was watching how the treatment was progressing before wandering off to snatch a bit of hay with his teeth from a small stack near the door. Other animals approached, though none got as close to Josh as the fearless pony. All the barn residents seemed interested at one point or another in what was going on in the formerly empty stall.

A short while later, the calf's leg was set, and Grace bounded up, clicking her tongue to attract Mergatroid's attention. The pony acted more like a faithful dog, prancing up to Deena for a pat on the head when she exited the stall. Mergatroid followed Grace back to the small homemade cart that sported bicycle tires and was custom made to the pony's low height.

"I have to get back. I've got chores still to do," Grace explained as she hitched the eager pony to the cart. Mergatroid was already heading towards home when Grace jumped aboard the cart, waving as she went back the way she'd come, over the grass tracks between cultivated fields.

Deena came up beside Josh, watching the young girl and the perky pony take off.

"Well, that did it. Every neighbor in the valley will know you're here by tomorrow night," Deena observed.

"But I thought the Amish didn't have phones?" Josh asked, turning toward her and seeking her gaze.

She smiled at him. "Who needs phones when you have a professional grade grapevine? You'll see. We might get a few visitors tomorrow. The neighbor ladies will probably drop by with innocent excuses to check you out and see if everything is in order around here."

"In order?"

"That we're not living in sin or getting up to ungodly hijinks." She chuckled as she said it, turning back toward the barn.

"And what if we were?" Concerned, he followed her into the barn and over to the stall where the calf was now resting comfortably.

Josh stopped short when he saw the resident cow, Maisy, had found her way into the stall and had lain down behind the calf, so it could snuggle against her warm, furry side. Deena's animals were really something. Independent thinkers with a compassionate streak that was pretty obvious if you observed them for a while.

"I don't want to get you in trouble with your neighbors, Deena," he told her in a quiet voice, not wanting to disturb the bovine bonding that was taking place a few feet away.

"It'll be fine," she said. "Just be polite and stay outdoors, working. Woodwork is preferable. They respect men who know carpentry. The Amish never stop working, and they appreciate industriousness in others. I'll handle the nosy questions."

Josh was silent as Deena moved back into the stall to check on the little calf. He left her to her healing work and decided retreat was the better part of valor at the moment.

They dined together in her kitchen that evening. The meal was plain but bountiful, and Josh realized Deena must have gone to some trouble to prepare so much food. He saw the way she lived. Simply. She kept a huge kitchen garden and seemed to live off the land. She'd told him the neighbors kept her supplied with things she couldn't produce herself, and he saw evidence of that on the supper table.

He was certain, for instance, that she'd never had one of her animals butchered, but there was a big roast in the center of the table. She'd probably served meat knowing his wolf was a predator and therefore a devout carnivore. He had the impression that she hadn't put the roast out for her own benefit, though she did eat a small slice.

Her thoughtfulness once again humbled him, but he didn't know how to thank her without making things awkward between them.

Scratch that. *More* awkward between them.

Ever since they'd kissed, that was almost all he could think about. Kissing her again. Taking it a little farther this time...if she'd let him.

After dinner, Deena went out to the barn to see to the animals and check on the calf before dark. Josh offered to help, but she politely declined. He had to work off some of his restless energy, so he decided to shift and take a prowl around the perimeter of Deena's property as night fell in earnest.

He had about an hour to kill before the moon would rise. He'd be sure to circle around to the standing stones just before so he could keep his promise to join Deena for the full moon ceremony she'd invited him to earlier.

He figured he'd go in his furry form, since the pull of the moon made it harder than usual to keep his human shape. He could participate in the ritual in either form, so it didn't matter much to him.

Though, if he was being honest with himself, going in wolf form was a bit of a test for Deena. So far, she hadn't really seen him in his fur.

Oh, she might've glimpsed him prowling out of the yard the night before, on his way to do a perimeter check, but she hadn't confronted him about it. He wasn't sure she would be entirely comfortable with the stark evidence of his dual nature, but if he was going to get involved with her any deeper, he had to know if his wolf side was going to pose a problem.

He didn't really know why it was so important, but it was. He could learn from anyone willing to teach, but if he was going to get involved on a more personal level, he didn't want there to be any question of her acceptance of his wolf.

For not only was his human mind nearly consumed with thoughts of kissing her again, but his wolf half was starting to have very serious thoughts about the future. With her. A future where the wolf ran in the cornfield behind this very farm, hunting unseen prey—or anything that might pose a danger to Deena. The wolf was feeling protective. *Very* protective. And more than a little possessive.

The thought should have frightened him, but it didn't. In fact, it felt right. Comforting. Almost inevitable.

The wolf was thinking…*mate*.

CHAPTER FIVE

Deena hadn't seen Josh since just after dinner, but she knew he was around. She could feel his presence in the woods that hid the stone circle from casual observance. The magic infused into the earth in this place was mostly what kept non-magic folk from seeing it, but the surrounding trees did their part as well.

Deena came out just before the moon was set to rise and felt the stones welcome her as they always did. She felt lighter within their sheltering circle, yet also more grounded to Mother Earth. It was a bit of a paradox, but it also made a perfect kind of sense to her magical perceptions. She went about her preparations as usual. There wasn't much she needed inside the circle. In fact, she could do this ritual just about anywhere, with no props at all, and it would still be valid and true.

The fact that she'd been gifted this sacred spot when she'd been granted guardianship of this land—however temporary—meant that she could do more. *A lot* more, if the occasion warranted it. For tonight, however, she would keep things simple.

A chalice of pure water. A lit candle, the flame dancing merrily into the cool evening breeze. Her athame—a dagger-like knife inscribed with powerful runes of magic and protection—and a few other things. Some herbs, salt, a few small semi-precious gemstones. She placed all these things around the stone circle in places of honor and power, keeping the chalice, candle and blade with her in the center, on the low slab of living rock that served as an altar stone.

Moments before she was set to begin, as the moon just began to make its appearance on the distant horizon, she felt Josh's presence. He prowled into the circle on silent paws, startling her a little. She realized almost immediately how foolish her reaction had been and tried to regulate her appearance and heartbeat. Why shouldn't a werewolf show up in wolf form?

Actually, now that she thought about it, she realized he'd been practicing restraint. Either that or he'd been hiding his wolf form from her until this moment. She'd known he'd been roaming her land in his four-footed guise, but aside from the occasional glimpse of his fur as he bounded away, she hadn't really seen his predator form out in the open like this.

She looked across the low stone altar where Josh sat on his haunches opposite her. His wolf eyes held every bit of the intelligence that she had seen in his human gaze. He watched her closely, even though his head was bowed, just slightly to the side, in what she took for respect.

"Welcome, forest lord," she said, using the proper words that she had been taught years ago but hadn't used in a very long time. It wasn't often that she had guests of any kind at her rituals, and half-fey werewolves were a rarity indeed.

The wolf's head nodded in acknowledgment, Josh's steady gaze never leaving hers. He sat waiting, watching her…almost unnerving her, but she refused to give in to nervous jitters. What did she have to be nervous about? She'd done this ceremony thousands of times, yet something about her guest was making her uneasy in her own skin. Not in a bad way. It was more like she was hypersensitive—overly alert to every little sound and motion. Hyper-aware of the handsome man-turned-beast watching her every move.

He was making her self-conscious! She almost shook her head, realizing how much of a ninny she was acting. It was like she was a teenager all over again or something. A cute boy was looking at her, and suddenly, she was all thumbs. She would have laughed at herself if she could have gotten away with it.

Instead, she took a deep breath and refocused her mind on the task at hand. She started the ceremony as the moon began to travel up into the sky. After a few minutes, the words and rituals fell into their familiar rhythm. She was calm. She was at peace with the world and expressing her gratitude to the Mother of All, honoring Her and all Her creation.

The ritual felt especially poignant this night, and somewhat wild. That was probably due to Josh's presence in the circle, his untamed magic and more primitive form lending something special to the ceremony. The magic that rose inside the shelter of the standing stones was more intense than usual, and when the rite reached its peak along with the moon, the force of power that poured forth as a blessing upon the Earth and all of the Mother's creation was more than Deena had expected—or experienced—in a very long time.

Josh howled, making her jump, but she knew the magic of the stone circle would contain the wolf's howl. Neighbors wouldn't be combing the woods, looking to kill the predator. Thank the Goddess.

No, the howl was something exuberant. A wild expression of Josh's wolf nature. It was a blessing in itself, from the most primitive part of him. A call of greeting and thanks to the Mother of All that reverberated through Deena's bones and down into her soul.

She concluded the ceremony shortly after, pleased with the night's turn of events.

As the magic she had called began to dissipate, a new wilder magic seemed to rush in to fill the void in the circle. Deena realized with alarm that it was coming from Josh. His fey magic pulsed out of him, knocking his wolf form to the ground. He looked as if he was in distress, so Deena rushed around the altar to check on him.

The moment she touched his fur, sparks flew, spiraling up into the cone of power contained by the ring. As before, her magic met his, and visible points of light resulted, but this time, they were epic. Trails of bright, rainbow-colored speckles swirled around them, piggybacking on the magic of her earlier benediction, following it upwards, into the heavens, toward the majestic full moon.

Deena knew Josh wasn't doing this on purpose. Something inside him—that newfound magic he didn't know how to control—had been called to the surface by the full moon ritual, and the overflow was venting itself skyward. She'd been teaching him how to control it, but apparently, it was still too soon for him to have completely overcome the mad rush of power that he'd been experiencing since his fey side woke.

Under her hands, his fur turned to flesh as he shifted to his human form unexpectedly. His *naked* human form. She went from stroking his furry wolf back to stroking his hard-muscled, sexy, human back. The tingle of their combined magic warmed her fingers, but the more she touched him, the more familiar and pleasant the energy became.

Interesting. And exciting in ways she hadn't wanted to contemplate in a very long time.

"Are you okay?" she asked him in a soft tone, concerned by his reaction to the ceremony.

He shook his head, leaning to the side so he could roll to a sitting position. He'd been on all fours, an echo of the wolf's standing position, but he moved to a more human pose now that he was wearing his two-legged form.

"Sorry. I'm not sure what just happened," he admitted, not meeting her eyes.

"I think…" She reluctantly stopped touching him and sat down beside him on the ground. "I think it was just a little too much stimulation, too soon. I'm sorry. I should've foreseen that the way this circle concentrates power might trigger something."

He did look up at her then, swiveling his head to the side, though his neck was still bent. "It's not your fault, Deena. You have nothing to be sorry for. I just need to get better at controlling this new energy. It's still wild, but not like my wolf. The wolf is wild, but reasonable. This…" He shook his head again. "There's no rhyme or reason to it. The wolf always has a reason for his actions. Hunger, anger, play, whatever. This new magic doesn't seem to have that kind of consciousness behind it."

She was silent a moment, thinking through his words. Something important was happening here.

"I think it's because your fey side should be controlling it, but you've never been aware of your fey nature. You still think like a human."

"I *am* human, dammit!"

That came out louder than she'd expected, and she was afraid she'd said the wrong thing, but he sighed and seemed to relax after a moment.

"I'm sorry," he apologized. "I don't mean to take this out on you. Heaven knows, it's not your fault. Nothing is your fault. You're trying to help me. It's just all so frustrating."

"I get it." She reached out to put one hand on his shoulder. The tickle of their energy meeting was gentler this time as they seemed to get used to each other's power. "I just wish I could make this easier for you. You might still be part human, but your mother has to be mostly shifter, right? And that's how you were raised—thinking you were the product of a human-shifter mating. But, Josh, judging by the sheer intensity of your magic, your dad had to have been fey. At this point, you know the wolf better than you know the fey part of your nature, and I think that's what's causing the imbalance." She thought about her words and the hypothesis she'd come up with, then added the qualifier. "Maybe."

Silence fell as he seemed to think over her words, and she realized she'd been holding something back from him that she really shouldn't have. Sharing her own dual nature wasn't something she did as a rule, but Duncan had sent Josh here for the very simple reason that Deena knew more about balancing fey magic than others because she, herself, was part fey.

It was time to come clean.

"You know..." she began, not really sure how to start this topic. "I told you I was in exile out here because of my ability to act as a channel for the Goddess, but there's a reason I'm such a good conduit."

She took a deep breath, sensing his stillness and his attentive stance, even though he wasn't looking at her. It felt like he was holding his breath, wondering what she would say. Somehow, he was able to read her feelings and probably sensed how important her words were to her—how she wouldn't share what she was about to say lightly.

He didn't prompt her or prod her. He just waited. Patient with her reluctance and willing to let her go at her own pace. He respected her. That's what it boiled down to, she realized with a feeling of warmth in her heart. She hadn't known how much she wanted his respect until that moment.

"You see, Josh…"

She turned to look at him. Slowly, his gaze rose to meet hers, and she could see the patterns of tempestuous golden energy in his eyes. It made her breath catch at such visible evidence of his inner power and the struggle to contain it. She was glad they were inside the stone circle, where any explosions of energy would be better contained than if they were out in the open.

"Don't worry. I've got it under control for now. What you said about my fey side helped me figure out a few things just now," he told her. The fact that he was trying to reassure her when he was the one in trouble touched her heart.

"I can help more. It's why Duncan sent you to me. Josh, I'm part fey too. My grandmother is fey, and her power passed down to me in such a way that leaves me more open to the distant realms of existence—including the fey realm—than pretty much anyone else on Earth. My dedication to the Goddess allows me to use this unique gift, but the Mother of All also protects me from some of the darker energies that might otherwise find their way into this world through me."

Josh's eyes flared for a moment, then the swirling energy in them quieted down as he looked at her. His expression was full of compassion, which was something she hadn't quite expected from the badass werewolf.

"Oh, honey. You've got it worse than I do, and here I am on your doorstep complaining and acting like an ass. I'm sorry."

He reached out and tugged her into his arms in a move she couldn't anticipate. She reminded herself that most shifters were tactile beings, and she'd been told they often touched each other to offer silent support. Hugs were common among them, she supposed, but she couldn't stop thinking about the fact that he was naked, and she was very aware of his bare chest as he held her.

"You have nothing to apologize for, Josh. I've had all my life to learn to deal with this. I've had the best training from the time I was a child, and all the help I could want or need from my family and the Goddess Herself. I've been blessed many times over while you've had to do it all on your own, and in a fraction of the time." She looked up at him, staring deep into his eyes. "You need my help now, and I'm glad to give it. I'm just sorry I didn't understand the true nature of the problem sooner. I don't talk about my fey side with anyone besides my family, and I don't see them as much as I used to. I'm not usually comfortable laying it all out there."

"Totally understandable," Josh said, nodding. "If the bad guys knew about you, you'd probably be even more of a target than

I am. I get that. And, after all, I'm new here."
He smiled, and his words were spoken in a
deep, soft, almost sexy tone that started a
little fire deep inside her. "You needed to get
to know me and be sure that I'm not on the
wrong side of things before you could trust
me. Don't apologize for being cautious. It
could save your life."

"I should have known you were okay
when the Lady spoke to you. She wouldn't
have shown Herself to an enemy, or even to
a neutral. She only appears to those firmly
on the side of Light."

"Don't be so sure," he cautioned her.
"She told me I'd be tested, and if I came out
on the right side of things, we'd talk further.
I think She was reserving judgment on me."

"She said that to you? Really?" Deena was
surprised by Her message.

"You aren't aware of what She says when
she takes over your body?" Josh asked, his
expression curious.

Deena shook her head, moving a few
inches back from him. "Not a word. My
spirit goes on vacation into another realm
while the Lady speaks. I don't hear what She
says unless She wants me to hear it.
Whatever was said between you and Her, is

strictly between the two of you."

"That's kind of fascinating." He was staring at her now, his lips curving upward in a smile. "I won't pretend to know how any of this stuff works, but I find it very compelling. I mean, I've always believed in the Goddess, but I had no real concept of how…present…She is in our lives. I never had much time for spiritual things before the magic hit."

"It awakened," she corrected him gently. "When you needed it most, your magic came suddenly alive within you, and I'm not surprised you're having a hard time dealing with it. Josh, you're much closer to your fey ancestor than I am. I mean, I call her my grandmother, but fey are basically immortal, and the liaison that produced my line is pretty ancient. There are a lot of *greats* that belong in front of the word grandmother in my case, but your fey ancestor was your father. You're truly half fey, and for whatever reason, your fey magic was sequestered until you were threatened by those mages and that somehow triggered its release all at once. That must've been truly scary."

"You have no idea." Josh shook his head,

removing one arm from around her so that they sat companionably side by side, his remaining arm around her shoulders. "Luckily, I was in the middle of nowhere when it happened. Nobody else around for miles. Otherwise, I might've attracted even more attention, or killed someone else—someone innocent—with the lightning storm I generated. It was intense."

She chuckled with him. "Judging by the level of your energy, I can only imagine. You're very strong, in case you were wondering. I have to really work, sometimes, to find my magic and use it. When the Goddess comes, of course, it's a different story, but if I'm trying to do something on my own—something not associated with Her—it can be hard. I don't think you'll ever have that problem. Your magic roils very close to the surface. I can feel it from across the room, and as close as we are now, I can sense the nearly unbridled intensity of your power. Duncan was right to send you here. You need to get control of that monster inside you—and I'm not talking about the wolf. He's a fluffy puppy compared to your fey side."

That startled a laugh out of him. "I don't

think I've ever been called a puppy before," he mused, still chuckling.

"A *fluffy* puppy," she repeated, laughing with him.

CHAPTER SIX

"I'd be insulted if I didn't understand what you meant. The first time the fey magic came out, it scared the crap out of me. After it was all over, I went wolf and ran and ran across the canyons and buttes, but I finally realized I couldn't outrun it. I couldn't outrun myself." His humor was gone. "And then, the chase really started, and for the first time in my life, I was the prey." His expression darkened as he stared out at the stone circle.

"That can't have been comfortable for your wolf."

He blew out a breath, shaking his head. "You can say that again. It's been kind of chaotic ever since, and really bloody. So far,

I've been able to defeat all those who have tried to steal my power, but some of those battles were too close for comfort, and I honestly don't know what I'm doing when it comes to the new magic. I was damned lucky a few times that it struck out in the right way to help the situation, but at other times, I've been caught totally clueless on how to get it to either join in the battle or help protect my back. It's like it was sitting, watching, almost mocking my efforts."

"Now that's one thing you've got to stop right away," she told him, seeing something she could help with. "It's not separate from you, even though it feels that way because it's new to you. Thing is, it was there all the time, within you. It *is* you. You have to embrace that and accept it on a fundamental level. I bet those times when the magic aided you were situations where you weren't thinking too hard about it. Maybe there wasn't even time to think. You just reacted to the threat and used everything inside of you to answer it."

He looked pensive. "Yeah. I think maybe you might be on to something there."

"Good." She smiled over at him. "That's something we can work on. A place to start, at least."

"You've already taught me a lot, Deena." His voice dropped to a low, intimate tone, and the swirling patterns of magic in his eyes slowed to a seductive blaze that almost mesmerized her.

She saw him moving closer and could easily read his intentions. He was going to kiss her, and she was going to allow it. No. Not just allow it. She was going to revel in it.

She'd been wanting him to kiss again almost from the moment their first kiss had ended. She leaned closer, inviting the kiss she had been anticipating, happy the time had finally arrived for their lips to meet again.

His mouth claimed hers, and this time, there was no stopping. No brakes. Nothing to hinder them. He was already naked, and they were within the loving protection of the Goddess's own stone circle. They were as safe as they could possibly be.

They were in their own little world with nothing but the feel of his hot skin under her hands and the taste of his kiss, and the hardness of his desire, so evident as he took her to the soft earth in front of the low stone altar.

The interior of the circle was always clean and lush with plant life. The Goddess's magic kept it glowing with greenery and the occasional flower, though in winter such things weren't visible unless you were within the circle. And the circle itself wasn't visible to non-magical folk at all.

Josh lay her on her back, coming down over her as he took full possession of her mouth. She moaned as she felt the warmth of him blanketing her from above. He kept the vast majority of his solid weight off of her, leaning up on his arms, but she still felt surrounded—encompassed—in his embrace, his hands on the ground on either side of her head.

The kiss went deeper, his tongue staking a claim on her that she could not deny. She didn't *want* to deny him anything. She wanted it all. With Josh.

The attraction was raw and powerful. Just like his magic. Something in him had called out to her from the first. Something primal. Even more basic than his wolf nature. This was magic primeval, his energy calling to hers, his spirit finding a connection with hers in a way that was both unique and utterly fascinating.

"Do you want me?" Josh broke off kissing her to ask. "Do you want this? Us?"

His magic was still very near the surface, but it was more controlled now. More patient and pensive. It was waiting for her answer. *He* was waiting for her answer.

Did she want to make love to Josh? *Oh, yeah.*

She nodded at him, unable to form the words for a moment. This felt big. Momentous. Life-altering.

But did it feel that way to him, as well? She couldn't be sure. Did it really matter right at this very moment?

She convinced herself it didn't. There would be time later to carefully consider her actions, but right now, all that mattered was his hands on her body, his body joining to hers. Pleasure promised and received. Given and taken in equal measure. She wanted that with all her heart, and she knew, without fully understanding how she knew, she would get that from this encounter. This man. This special moment out of time.

"Yes," she managed to say, holding his gaze and wondering if he felt how the world had changed with that single word.

"Yes?" he repeated, as if unsure he'd

heard her correctly.

She nodded again. "Yes, Josh." Her words were coming more easily now that she'd crossed the hurdle of making up her mind. "I want to be with you. Now. Here."

A smile started in his sparkling eyes and stretched his lips. It warmed her, even as she saw the satisfaction of his inner predator, having cornered his prey. But the wolf meant her no harm. She knew that instinctively. No, the wolf that shared Josh's soul had been stalking her for days, she realized suddenly. The wolf had wanted her for a while and was satisfied with a hunt well played.

She would have laughed had the situation not been so potentially explosive. Josh's hands on her body were making her squirm as he divested her of her clothing…slowly…gently…intently.

Her own magic gathered, pushed against her skin, wanting to get out. The magic wanted to romp with the answering energy in Josh's soul. It wanted to caress him the way his wild magic caressed her with his every touch.

She'd never experienced anything like it before. Then again, she'd never made love to a half-fey werewolf before. The flavor of his magic was heady. Powerful and wild. Nascent, yet fully developed, and his fey side was even stronger than hers in its intensity. The feel of their magics blending was heady stuff. She almost felt drunk on the simple touches they'd exchanged to this point. She wondered what would happen when they climaxed. Supernova? She was almost afraid to find out, but nothing was going to stop this. Not now.

Her fears of the unknown. His uncertainty about his feyness. All of that meant little when he was undressing her. Stroking each inch of skin he uncovered. Laying kisses down on each part of her body he exposed.

He paused at her breasts, licking and sucking, squeezing and rubbing. Her breath grew short as she panted, and her excitement rose to new heights. Her clothing disappeared, and she lost track of where he threw the various items. It didn't matter. Nothing mattered except the two of them, here and now.

She tried to stroke him the way he was stroking her, but he wouldn't allow much contact. He made her feel as if this was all for her. That she was the center of his universe at this moment and that her pleasure was paramount. She wanted to give equal measure, but he moved away from her seeking hands and diverted her with new moves that made her moan with desire.

The man was a menace. A skilled lover who seemed to know every trick in the book to make her forget all about her plans to cover him in kisses and make her impatient for him to fill her with his hardness so they could ride to the stars together. She was through waiting. She wanted to feel him inside her.

"Do me now, Josh," she breathed, clutching his shoulders as he made room for himself between her splayed thighs. "Come into me now. No more waiting." Her words were ragged puffs of whispered air, but he seemed to hear. And obey.

He pushed into her, going slowly at first. He was a big man, and she hadn't done this in far too long. She had to adjust, and he gave her all the time she needed to do so. But then... As soon as they were both comfortable, he began to move.

And the Earth itself moved. Or at least, it seemed to from her perspective. Almost immediately, pleasure zinged through her. It was a small climax compared to what came next, but it stole her breath and made her realize she'd never been with a man who cared so much for her before. Josh was truly special. In so many ways.

He rode her through the initial peaks and pushed her ever higher. He was a considerate lover, not rushing her or pushing her too hard. But he was also an animal at heart. At least part of him was a wolf spirit, and that wolf both cared for its mate—or at least the woman it was mating with at the time—and drove them both toward climax. Relentlessly. With the wildness that was part of his soul.

At the same time, Deena was very aware of the way their magics were building up. Merging and parting. Converging with almost explosive strength, then moving away as if repelled. At one point, they joined together, and she wasn't entirely sure that, when the magic separated again, it was as purely one or the other as it had been. It certainly felt like a little bit of his primeval nature had joined to her human-fey magic, and a bit of her seemed to be part of him now. Unless she was much mistaken.

But those thoughts were for another time.

She would ponder it all later. There were probably unexpected ramifications to what she believed might have just happened, but they were in the Goddess's circle, under Her protection. Whatever happened here would probably work out for the best. At least, she hoped so.

And then, there was no more time for thinking as the world spun apart in the brightest climax yet. Josh tensed above her as he cried out, coming to his own completion, even as she shook with reaction, her body spasming in the most amazing pleasure she had ever known.

They clung to each other as the intensity of the orgasm washed over them both. At one point, she opened her eyes to see the sacred circle lit with a billion particles of the purest white light, reaching up toward the heavens as if to add to the collection of stars already there.

That was their magic. The combination of their energies was as explosive as she'd suspected it would be, but the unexpected purity of the bright white light was something she could not ever had guessed at. It was significant in ways that she could spend a lifetime pondering, but for right now, she was just happy to be here, sharing this moment, with one of the most intriguing men she had ever encountered.

"You okay?" His voice was a sexy low growl near her ear.

He'd collapsed partially over her, though the bulk of his considerable weight was to her side. Their legs were still tangled together, but he'd managed to move most of his torso off her before his strength gave out.

She looked over at him and smiled. "I'm wonderful." Her words were slurred with bliss, slow with lethargy he'd induced by scrambling her pleasure receptors and turning her mind to mush in the best possible way.

He smiled back. "Me too." He rolled slightly, landing beside her, on his back, gazing upward at the last of the little white sparkles of their energy floating heavenward. "Did we cause that?" he asked, pointing to the fading energy that was still strong enough to be visible from within the magical confines of the stone circle.

"Mm-hmm," she replied, feeling both satisfied and oddly proud. "It was even more intense a few minutes ago."

"You bet it was."

She chuckled at his humor. "I'll second that, but I was talking about the energy floating up to the universe."

He played innocent. "So was I. Scout's honor."

She looked over at him, narrowing her eyes. "Were you ever a scout?"

"No, but I've been known to hide out in the woods near the scout camps. At least I know scouts won't indiscriminately start shooting at a lone wolf in the woods."

A comfortable silence fell for a few moments.

"It must be so cool to be able to become a wolf," she said, not realizing she was about to reveal that particular thought out loud. It seemed all her defenses were down after the amazing experience of making love with Josh.

Not that she minded that he now knew how cool she thought shapeshifting was. On the contrary, of all her inner conjectures to come out unexpectedly, that was probably the least embarrassing.

"It is," he agreed. "It can also be dangerous under the wrong circumstances."

"I bet," she agreed. "But still... To have

heightened senses must be neat. Or gross, I guess, at times."

"Nothing really grosses out my wolf side. Nature is nature. The only thing that really bothers me is the scent of certain harsh chemicals and really strong odors that don't exist in nature. Excessive noise gets to me, too, which is why cities are difficult."

"But not impossible, right? I mean, you had to have gone to New York to meet Duncan, and I know there are Packs of wolves who live there."

"Yeah, I ran afoul of one while I was looking for Duncan. I hate wolf Packs." His voice had turned to a growl that surprised her.

"Really? Why?" He'd surprised her with his attitude toward other wolves.

"All those petty rules," he replied. "All that formality and one-upmanship."

"Spoken like the wolf who knows he has no equal," she complimented him, realizing how hard things must've been for him all this time, not really knowing the other side of his nature. "I can see where it would've been tough for you. All that magic bottled up inside... You must've known instinctively that there was more, but you didn't know how to get to it."

He rolled his head over to meet her gaze. "Maybe." Then, he turned to look starward again. "I can't really say what screwed up my past, but now that I've met you and am learning about all this stuff..." He gestured toward the last little sparks of white light that were just visible as they made their way out into the universe. "I have hope for a better future for possibly the first time in my life. If I haven't said it before, thank you for that, Deena. And for so much more. You're a pretty amazing woman."

She felt like preening under his praise. His words made her feel all warm and fuzzy, though she wasn't very good at accepting compliments.

"I'm glad you think so, because I think you're a pretty amazing guy," she told him, feeling a little shy, even after their incredible sexual encounter.

"You do?" His tone was back to teasing as he rolled onto his side, propping his head up on one hand. "Then, what do you say to continuing this inside? On a softer surface? With sheets?"

The light dancing in his eyes now was tamed. Happy and not as chaotic as the golden swirling light she'd seen before. Their encounter had changed him. It had changed his energies, subduing his power in a good way, making order out of the chaos. At least for now. Perhaps the change would be long-term, but there was no way to know that at this point.

Still, any change from that explosive, tempestuous energy was good. This was a step in the right direction, for sure. She smiled with happiness, both for his progress—even though he didn't realize it just yet—and his suggestion that they go inside and try this again. As far as she was concerned, she had nothing but him on her agenda for the rest of the night.

CHAPTER SEVEN

When Josh woke the next morning, he was alone in the king-sized bed in the guest room of Deena's house. They'd retired to his room because she'd told him shyly that it had the bigger bed. He liked that her room wasn't a siren's lair. He felt a primitive sort of satisfaction that she didn't sleep with every man that came calling. Not that she seemed to get a lot of company way out here.

Still, his inner caveman liked to imagine her sleeping all alone in her bower...until he rolled into town. The wolf inside him wanted to howl in satisfaction while his two-legged side just wanted to laugh at his own thoughts.

Sometime in the night—in the collision and blending of their magical energies—he'd become hyper-aware of the luscious feel of Deena's power. He could truly appreciate now how it lay just under the surface, an inferno of strength, linked through Deena's beautiful soul to the Goddess Herself.

No wonder the Mother of All found it easy to speak through Deena. Her soul was the purest Josh had ever encountered, and her strength was awesome in its ferocity, with the flavor of other realms. Perhaps, in time, he'd learn to control his newly awakened magic as Deena could.

He already felt better about his wayward power. It seemed more willing to obey his wishes this morning. As if it had learned from the merger with Deena's last night.

Reaching out with just a tiny tendril of his power, Josh tried to figure out where Deena had gone. Judging by the faint light slanting in through the window blinds, it was early morning. Very early. Just the other side of dawn.

Then, he realized. She'd probably gone down to the barn to see to her friendly animals. He encountered her energy more easily than he'd expected—this being a new skill and something he'd never really tried before. If he interpreted his magical senses correctly, she was checking on the injured calf, who had spent the night with Deena's other animals, surrounded in a furry, protective circle.

He had to marvel at how Deena's mismatched family of animals seemed to cross species lines easily. The alpacas had allowed the little calf to snuggle into their wool as they sat, one on each side of the baby. That was the picture in Deena's mind when Josh made light contact. The sense of love and happiness that filled her spilled over and made him feel lighter.

When she became aware of him, the feelings intensified, as if she were sending them to him, and he found himself with one hand clutched to his heart. Not in pain, but in wonder. He'd never felt such things before. Only with this special, magical woman.

She managed to communicate the idea that she'd see him soon. He interpreted the emotional tone to mean that she'd finish with her menagerie and then come back to the house.

Josh leapt out of bed and cleaned himself

up, dressing with extra care, though his wardrobe didn't really give him a lot of choices. Clean jeans and T-shirt was about as far as he could go. But he could definitely get breakfast started in the kitchen. His inner wolf growled agreement about feeding their female. They had to take care of her. She was *theirs*.

Such possessive thoughts didn't scare him anymore. In fact, it didn't even make him blink. Somewhere in the night, he'd accepted his fate. Not only *accepted* it, but looked forward to the time when she would understand that what they'd shared had been for keeps. They were mates.

Josh was just putting breakfast on the table when he heard a scuffling sound that seemed out of place. He'd been keeping his wolf-enhanced senses alert to keep track of Deena's progress through the barn. He could just hear her murmur to various members of her menagerie and their vocal responses. A whicker from a horse. A gentle moo from the cow. A kind of chittering sound from the furry alpacas. Clucks from chickens, honks from geese, quacks from ducks, and the like.

He'd timed his breakfast service with what he'd thought was the sounds of her washing up with the hose out in the yard as she finished her morning rounds, when the new sound intruded. It was coming from the road near the front of the house, and it didn't sound friendly.

All the animals had gone quiet.

The backdoor opened even as Josh headed toward the front.

"Wait," Deena said in an urgent whisper. "Someone's testing my wards."

"Visitors?"

"No," she answered distractedly. "Invaders."

Josh paused, frowning at her. "Can they get through?"

She shrugged, still seeming to concentrate on something elsewhere. "Eventually."

"Do we stand our ground or run?" That was the crux of the matter as far as he was concerned.

"Can't run. The animals would be unprotected. I'll stand and fight."

His wolf liked the determined look on her face, even as his human side worried that she might be in danger. He didn't like the way she'd phrased her defiance, though. He was with her. He'd be fighting at her side. He wouldn't leave her on her own to defend her animals and home.

"Once they're inside your perimeter, is there a spot you prefer for the fight? Do we give up any ground?" he asked experimentally, feeling out her strategy.

"Not if I have anything to say about it." She narrowed her eyes and looked straight at him. "I could use your help, though."

"Whatever you need." His answer was immediate and definite. He'd give anything to protect her—up to, and including, his life.

"I guess all that magic last night didn't go unnoticed, though I thought the majority of it had been contained by the stone circle," Deena thought aloud as she braced herself for yet another testing of her wards.

The wards themselves weren't meant to keep anything serious out. They were her early warning system, and they stood firm against most intrusions, but if real power came against them, they would fail. And it felt like they were on the verge of failure right now.

"Whoever's out there, he's strong. Very strong. And not friendly."

A growling sound came from Josh's throat—a sharp reminder that her ally was not fully human or fey, but was also a werewolf. She wondered if that would help them against what was coming. She thought maybe it could be used to their advantage. Somehow.

"Which direction?" he barked, though she knew his harsh tone wasn't directed at her.

"He's coming in from the front. The ward is about to come down across the drive, and I sense him just waiting to drive down it. He's got a motor running of some sort. Maybe a car. Or maybe a motorcycle. I can't be sure."

Josh paused a second, his ear tilted toward the front of the house. "Motorbike," he told her. "Though there's noise out on the road, too, so I can't be certain that's all he has, but there is one dirt bike type engine idling in the area next to your mailbox."

"Nice." She took a moment to compliment his superior hearing.

"I'm going to go out and scout. If he makes it down the drive, either stay in the house or go out the back. You'll be stronger in the standing stones, right?"

Josh was really taking charge, and she wasn't sure if she liked it or not. He wasn't asking her opinion, except on the small matter of the circle, but now was not the time to argue. The wards were about to go. She could feel it.

But he was right about the stones protecting her. "I'll go for the stone circle," she told him. "Nothing can touch me there. But you should come with me."

"I'll meet you there," he promised, but she sensed he wouldn't seek the safety of the stones until the danger was dealt with. He was planning to face the enemy alone, which didn't sit right with her. Not at all.

She was about to argue with him when she felt the wards fall. Her knees almost went out from under her, but she clutched the back of a chair to steady herself. She caught Josh's concerned gaze.

"What just happened? Was that the ward?" he asked. He must have felt something when the magical barrier dissipated, but he didn't know enough about the subject yet to know for sure.

"The wards are down," she confirmed.

"Then, we're out of time. Go for the circle. I'll be right behind you."

Again, she wanted to argue with him, but the roar of an engine coming down to drive stopped her. He gave her one last long look, filled with meaning, and things they had not yet said out loud, and then, he was out the door. He was going to face danger in her stead. That just irked the crap out of her, but at the same time, it was kind of romantic too.

Still, she wasn't about to let him fight her battles for her. If anything, they had probably attracted this danger together. Their lovemaking had set off sparks that had somehow captured the attention of exactly the wrong person, and he would have to be dealt with. By both of them. Together. Just as it had started.

Josh was already out the door, but she followed him. She was cautious, peering out before she committed herself to moving beyond the imagined safety of the doorway, but Josh was already out of sight. His natural shifter stealth made him impossible to see unless he wanted to be seen, she was sure.

The motorbike raced up the driveway, the tinny sound of its engine assaulting her ears. It skidded to a stop, throwing dirt and gravel in a destructive wave before it, and even before the bike came to a halt, the man on its back was lobbing a dangerous ball of malevolent energy toward her with one hand.

"What? You don't even introduce yourself? You just break down my wards and start throwing your shit around like you own the place?" She screamed her insults at the man, even as she blocked his magical attack with a domed shield of pure energy that held his power at bay about ten feet from her.

"Forgive me," he said, his obnoxious tone sarcastic in the extreme. "I'm Reginald Park of the *Venifucus*, and now, your power will be mine." He threw his other hand up into the air and renewed his attack, but Deena was ready. Her shield bowed out, drawing a little closer to her body, but easily deflecting the man's magical energy around her, dissipating it into the earth and sky.

"Fat chance, Reggie!" she called back, taunting him into another attack. Better to drain off some of his energy in these first moves of the fight while she studied both his technique and his level of ability.

She didn't like the way he'd claimed to be part of the *Venifucus*. That ancient order of evil doers had been active in recent years, but she'd managed to stay under their radar for the most part. Still, she knew they were bad business.

Deena heard a growling sound off to her right a split second before Josh launched himself at Reggie. He took the evil bastard totally by surprise, which would have been great, if Reggie hadn't had a friend.

A trampy-looking woman hit Deena from behind with a blast of smoky magic that made Deena skid down the path to the barn on her butt. Deena recovered quickly, coughing a few times to clear her lungs of the woman's foul energy before she could change her shield's direction to fend off the girlfriend's attack.

The woman wore riding leathers in black with red piping. On anyone else, Deena might've admired the way they fit, but the clothing had two strikes against it. First, it was *leather*—which was something she didn't like anywhere near her sanctuary farm—and second, it was worn by a woman who had clearly chosen the wrong side in the fight of good versus evil.

That didn't change the fact that this strange woman had knocked Deena flat on her ass. She was still trying to regroup when an unexpected cavalry charge nearly made her cry. All of her animals—every last one—

flew, clopped or otherwise ran out of the barn to get between the leather-clad female and Deena.

Her rescued animals were putting themselves in the line of fire for her. She had known they liked her, of course, but she hadn't quite realized the depth of their caring and love.

Deena could do nothing other than extend her shield to encompass her animals, drawing on the power of the Goddess and the bonds Deena had forged with each and every one of the animal spirits that had lovingly rushed to her defense. And there was a new energy available to her too. A wild, wolfen energy. A fey-tinged sexual energy that she had come to know intimately the night before.

Josh.

CHAPTER EIGHT

The man who'd identified himself as Reginald Park hadn't come alone, and Josh had sensed it almost too late. As it was, he saw Deena go flying at the hands of the female mage, but he thought Deena would be okay for a few moments while he neutralized what his wolf recognized as the more dangerous of the two—the male.

Josh couldn't allow himself to be distracted, but he was momentarily stunned when he saw the animals race to Deena's defense. Good souls, he thought, as he squared off against the man.

"You won't succeed," Josh taunted the man while using every bit of knowledge and instinct about magic he had.

"What? You think you and the girl can stand against me and Felicia? We have decades of training and scores of magical duels to our credit individually and as a pair." He tilted his head to one side and smiled. "Though I will confess, I had planned to take the priestess on my own, but when I realized she had a new farmhand..." Reginald's tone was insulting, but Josh let it wash over him. Anger wouldn't help him control his magic. "I called in Felicia, just to even the numbers, though we still have the advantage of you magically, newbie."

Even as the man spoke, he launched more magical fireballs at Josh, but his shielding was as good as he could make it. Now, he was glad of the time Deena had spent teaching him the finer points of a strong shield. He hadn't really appreciated that lesson until just now.

"I may be new, but I'm stronger than you, Reggie. And I'm like nothing you've ever encountered before." With those words, Josh let just a little of his wolf nature out, shifting to a quasi-battle form. He was gratified when the mage's eyes widened.

Most strong werewolves spent a lot of time practicing what was known as the battle form. It was the stage in transformation between human and wolf that had inspired the nightmare visions and mythology surrounding werewolves. Though most of the legends were wrong in many respects, the image of an upright creature walking on two legs with massive claws, furry muscled arms and legs, and the dangerous snout of a wolf with sharp pointy teeth was pretty accurate.

Josh, though, wasn't just any normal werewolf. He could hold the shift at any point in his transformation. He'd perfected what he thought of as a quarter shift, where he still looked mostly human, but was slightly larger than his usual six-foot-two frame, maybe a little hairier, but with claws and fangs. He knew he looked like something out of a nightmare—even to most shifters—and the quarter shift had helped him win many a fight.

He took that quarter-form now and saw the familiar glint of fear in Reginald's eyes. Good. Josh would take any advantage in what he knew would be a battle to the death.

This was no polite duel to first blood. No. Reggie and Felicia had come here intent on capturing Deena and stealing her power.

They'd probably intended to just eliminate Josh, since it was pretty clear that Reggie have already discounted him...until just a few short moments ago.

"What the hell are you?" Reggie asked, his voice rising as he realized he had taken on more than he'd bargained for, and quite possibly more than he could chew.

"I'm your worst nightmare, Reg," Josh growled, launching an attack both physical and magical.

He closed in on Reggie, and the evil mage had to give ground. Satisfaction pulsed through Josh. He didn't like being prey—as he had been since the new magic showed up. For the first time in months, Josh felt like he should. Like the predator that shared his soul. A protector of his people. An aggressor, when needed. And a defender of innocence—which was a task he had appointed himself.

Hearing a growl as Josh launched himself at Reggie, Deena looked over to see that Josh was holding his own, but Deena dared not take any of Josh's magical energy to fight Reggie's girlfriend. She could feel him doing the same, leaving her magic untouched.

Another round of evil smoke came Deena's way, distracting her from the problem of whether they should use each other's magic or not. She had bigger fish to fry.

"Hey, Smokey," she called. "Is that all you got?" Maybe insulting the bad guys wasn't the greatest strategy, but it made Deena feel good to get a few verbal jibes in, no matter how childish.

"Deena Half-Fey, I've been looking for you all over the place. Don't you recognize me? I'm Felicia, the one who will bring you before the *Mater Priori* and gift her with your power. I am your doom." A cackling laugh joined another round of oily smoke, which seemed to be the way this witch delivered her power.

"Funny, you look more like a tramp than somebody's doom. Of course, I can't really see you clearly through all this nasty smoke." Deena waved her hand and pushed the evil vapors aside, shooing them away, into the atmosphere where they could harm none. "Oh, that's better," Deena said, smiling brightly at the woman who faced her.

The animals were still in the line of fire, though they were as safe as she could make them behind Deena's shield. Slowly, she became aware of each of them lending a little part of their earthly energy to hers. They weren't magical in the same way shifters were, but every living thing on the planet had some sort of spark within them. The wild beasts were closer to their natures than most, and they were trying to help her.

Oddly enough, it was working. Their earthen magic blended with her unique mix of fey and human, making her stronger. Which gave her an idea...

Deena turned her attention back to Josh. He was still fighting Reggie, but the action had moved a little closer to her and the animals. Good. If her theory proved correct, they'd be much better off fighting side by side—or back to back.

First, to test the theory. With silent apology, Deena reached for a small tendril of Josh's shifter-fey magic. It came more readily to her than she had expected, and she used it to bind her own magic into a tight ball of blazing white light that she lobbed at her foe.

The trampy girlfriend who thought she was doom winced and fell on her tush. Deena wanted to crow, but the battle wasn't nearly over yet. Still, she had a plan, and she had proof of concept. Mixing their energies worked better than standing apart. Now, she had to figure out how to alert Josh to the phenomenon.

Josh wanted to cheer when he saw the witch fall. He'd been aware of Deena's small power draw, and the unexpected multiplication of energy had a fantastic payoff. He had gone on the offensive with Reggie, but the man was strong. Very strong. And it wasn't as easy to really hurt him as some of the other mages Josh had fought in the recent past. Josh did his best to work his way over to Deena, knowing that if they were going to merge their energies, it would be much better to present a united front.

But getting to her side was easier thought than accomplished. Reginald was doing his best to keep Josh busy, and even though Josh had been studying hard and had spent the last few months defending himself against this guy's friends, Josh still wasn't an expert at wielding magical energy. Not as a weapon. He could defend himself well enough, but his best attacks were still mostly physical, not magical. And even in his quarter-shifted form, he couldn't get close enough to Reggie to do any real damage.

He was feeling the pain of the hits Reggie had managed to score. Josh was scorched in a few places, and his jeans were definitely singed. Dammit. He'd just gotten these jeans worn in the way he liked. Another reason to curse Reggie and the dirt bike he rode in on.

Pissed off and in pain, Josh fought his way over to Deena. He didn't dare take any of her magical energy away until he was close enough to guard her back. He refused to leave her with less power. She had enough of a fight on her hands with that leather-clad bimbo, Felicia. Although, Josh had to admit, when he had a moment to glance over at Deena's progress, she was more than holding her own, and now, she was even scoring points off the other woman, knocking her down and making her bleed.

What a woman. Deena was everything he could want in a mate…and more.

With that thought in mind and a smile of anticipation on his face, Josh doubled down. He had to get to her. And then, they could end all this bullshit and get to the good part.

It took a few minutes, but eventually, Josh got his wish. He approached from the side, keeping Reggie in front of him as Josh backed into Deena's presence. He knew she was well aware of him, and when they touched—his back meeting hers—sparks of welcome greeted him.

"It's about time," she groused, but he could hear the laugh in her voice. "Are you ready to end this debacle?"

"Your wish is my command, sweetheart," he replied, for the first time, actually having fun while fighting for his life.

Oh, this situation was serious, but how could Josh not smile when he was with the woman he loved?

And yeah, he'd thought the L-word. There it was. The truth that had become clear in the middle of the night as they lay together. He loved her. And he suspected she returned the sentiment, though she hadn't yet said anything. That would come, he was fairly certain, given time. Now, he just had to make sure they had the time together—a bright future where they could share so much.

This fight had to end, and it had to end now.

"Shall we?" he asked her, touching the place deep in their souls where they'd connected the night before. The place that was forevermore joined, one to the other.

Seeking and finding that well of immeasurable strength, they both let loose, simultaneously, at their opponents. Josh followed Deena's lead as she formed the magical energy into tight balls that flew with uncaring accuracy, taking Reggie and his gal pal down to the ground.

Knock out. Game over. Thanks for playing.

When the white sparks died down enough for them to see again, both Reggie and the woman were flat on their backs on the ground, either unconscious or dead. Josh didn't much care which at the moment. Just that they were no longer fighting.

He sagged against Deena's back as she sagged against him. They sort of wobbled down to the ground, each supporting the other so that they ended up sitting on the grass, back to back, weary to their bones. The fight had taken a lot out of them, but Josh felt the satisfaction of victory. Together, they'd defeated their opponents and lived to tell the tale.

"What now?" she asked when she finally found the strength to speak. "I don't think they're dead, so what do we do with them?"

She gestured weakly toward the fallen enemy.

"I'm not a fan of outright murder, but we need to figure out something that will both prevent them from coming at us again, and from telling any of their friends where to find us," he replied, thinking aloud.

"There is something my grandmother taught me…" Deena said in a quiet tone, as if mulling her thoughts over. "We'd probably have to get them to the stone circle, though."

"Do you think your animal friends will consent to carry them there for you?" Josh gestured toward the animals, which had decided on their own, apparently, to form a protective ring around them. He'd never seen the like, except on this crazy, wonderful sanctuary farm.

Deena straightened up, seeming to regain some strength, and turned to look at him. "That's a good idea."

"I'd offer to carry them one at a time, but my muscles feel kind of weird right now, and I'm not too proud to admit it. I've never had such an intense magic duel before. The adversaries I've faced up to now weren't nearly as powerful as these two."

"They were *Venifucus*," Deena said quietly as she worked her way slowly to her feet.

She seemed to be in better shape than he was, which made sense considering she was the one with all the magical experience. Still, it stung his pride a bit. The wolf prodded him to help her and protect her, but his two-legged side knew she was a capable woman who would be his equal, not his dependent. The wolf was just going to have to figure that out.

"I've heard the term, but I'm afraid I don't know much about it," he said, trying hard to stand up himself.

"They are an ancient order, dating back to first appearance of Elspeth, the Destroyer. They were her servants and her allies, devoted wholly to her evil. It was thought they had been defeated when she was banished to the farthest realms centuries ago, but in recent years, they've made a comeback. As, some fear, has she." Deena spoke as she walked over to a tan horse.

She stroked the horse's hide and reached up to whisper in his ear. Josh could just hear her murmuring to the horse, asking him for his help in carrying the two mages. The horse nodded his head, for all the world looking like he was saying yes, then trotted over to sniff at Reggie.

It didn't take too long to get the enemy mages onto the horse's back and transport them to the standing stones. Josh had regained most of his physical strength and was able to muscle them on and off the horse as needed while Deena steadied her equine friend. Both Reggie and the woman remained unconscious throughout, for which Josh was glad. He didn't really feel up to having another magical showdown at the moment—and probably wouldn't for at least a few days.

Deena directed him to place the mages on the low stone altar. There was just enough room for both of them to lie half-on the stone slab, their feet dangling off either end of the rectangular rock.

Josh stood at Deena's side, ready to assist her in any way she requested while she began to chant. He recognized some of the lilting language, though he didn't know what it all meant. She paused occasionally, to sprinkle water over the two on the altar or smudge their foreheads with dirt. He could feel her calling on the magic they now shared between them, but there was a third presence as well... A presence he'd felt before.

The Goddess was with them, and he knew, whatever was about to happen, it was going to be memorable. And potentially awesome in its intensity. Josh tried to mentally prepare himself as best he could, but there really was no way to prepare for encountering the divine.

CHAPTER NINE

Deena started her chant, realizing that since blending her energies with Josh's, she had more power than ever to call on. She had to consciously dial it back a little to keep control. It was a heady feeling.

Her purpose here was to drain the evil magic from these two mages and send it back to the Earth, where it would be absorbed and do no harm. She would leave these two with no power to speak of and, if she did this right, no memory of their evil ways. But first, she had to seek the Goddess's permission and agreement with the plan. Nothing could happen without Her approval, for She knew more about the true nature of all creatures than anyone. If She granted mercy, it would be wrong for Deena to do anything to them.

Seeking and receiving approval, Deena became the instrument of the Goddess's justice. The evil in these two would be purged.

She wasn't sure how long it took, but Deena didn't tire. Not with Josh at her side, feeding her energy. The Goddess was near as well, watching over them, directing the outflow of magic from the evil mages and helping it dissipate harmlessly.

When the deed was done, the two attackers remained unconscious on the slab of stone as their magical energies were forever dispersed. Deena felt better than she'd expected, her own magical power stronger than it had been before meeting and joining with Josh. She turned to him, walking into his arms for a hug. She really needed one right now, and he didn't disappoint.

He enveloped her in his arms, offering comfort without question. She was so blessed in that moment, to have found a man willing to fight at her side and hug her when the danger had passed. He let her be who she was, though he'd tried to keep her out of the fray at first. She didn't hold that against him. He had simply been trying to be protective. It was sweet, but she hoped he realized after what they'd just been through that she could take care of herself.

"What now?" he asked quietly, still holding her close. His arms felt so safe, so secure. She was loath to step away from the comfort they offered and get back to reality, but she knew there was still work to do.

"They'll be unconscious for a while, I think," she told him, not really sure what to do next. "Their magic has been drained for all time, and their memories of us taken away. It would be best if they were taken somewhere else before they woke up, but I can't think where we could put them that would be safe."

"For them or for us?" His tone was speculative, and he was smiling when she looked up at him. She felt her lips twitch upward in an answer grin.

"Both, if we can manage it."

Their gazes met and held for a long moment. So much had happened in so short a time. Life-altering stuff.

A rustling sound penetrated the peace of the moment, and Josh whirled, putting Deena slightly behind him. He was instantly on alert.

"Perhaps I can be of some assistance," a new voice said from just outside the stone circle.

Deena recognized that voice, though she hadn't heard it in quite a while. She peered out from behind Josh's broad shoulders.

"Duncan?"

She saw the fey man smile faintly as he moved closer. Now that the ceremony was over, he was able to enter the ring easily.

"Forgive my late arrival. I thought I'd been leading these two merrily away from your door, but they doubled back, and I didn't realize it quite in time. I'm glad you were able to deal with them on your own." Duncan stood to one side of the altar, looking down on the unconscious former-mages with sympathy in his gaze. "I can transport them away, if you wish."

"Away where?" Deena wanted to know.

"For now, to a safe house from which they cannot escape," he said casually. "I have some questions to ask them when they wake. Then, after we've learned all we can, and deal with a few other matters, I'll deliver each separately to places from which they can begin to rebuild their lives as non-magical beings."

"You sound like you've done this before," Josh mused.

"On occasion," Duncan admitted. "I have battled the *Venifucus* in the past and am truly sorry to have to do so again, but there it is." Duncan sighed, shaking his head. "You've both exceeded all expectations here. I was truly concerned for your safety going up against these two. Deena, the more I analyze it, the more I think the male was already here, checking out our home when I dropped Josh off. He followed me for a while, but he must've dropped back at some point to get the woman and come back here. I'm sorry I didn't realize what was going on in time to help."

"That's okay," Deena said, even as Josh bristled a bit. She liked her protective wolf, but she also knew how hard it could be sometimes to track mages that didn't want to be tracked. The fact that she hadn't known Reginald was stalking her even before Josh arrived was troublesome. "I'm glad Josh was here," she said. "From what Reggie said, it delayed the attack until he could get Felicia in to help, which bought us some time, and they weren't prepared for how strong Josh is."

"They were after you, first and foremost," Duncan agreed, nodding. "Josh was just going to be a bonus. You were lucky they didn't realize exactly who he was or how powerful he is. This could've gone the other way if they'd brought in even more reinforcements." Duncan sighed wearily. "As it was, they were quite a powerful team. It's good that they won't ever be able to reconstitute their strength. The dissociation ritual was well performed." He bowed respectfully toward Deena.

"So, how do we want to do this?" Josh asked. Deena knew they had a number of things to accomplish before they could rest.

"We need to rebuild at least a basic ward as soon as possible," Deena put in. She was tired, but she knew it would be best to get the wards back up and protecting her land and her animal friends as soon as possible.

"I can help with that, but I should remove these two first," Duncan said. "I don't often use this sort of magic because it's very visible, but after everything that just happened here, I doubt it will be noticed. And if it is, perhaps it'll confuse the trackers a bit."

With those somewhat confusing words, Duncan reached out to touch one hand of each of the unconscious pair. Deena could feel an intense magical spike a moment before Duncan and the two former mages just disappeared.

"Well, hell," Josh observed. "If the dude can just pop around wherever he wants, why did he make me sit for hours in a car to get here?"

But of course they both already knew the answer. Duncan's words made more sense in light of the enormous magical outlay his instantaneous travel must require. It left quite an aftershock, as well, which was something they could both feel reverberating around the stone circle long after he and the two former mages poofed out of sight.

"It's a fey thing, though I'm not sure if all of them can manage it. I certainly can't do it, even though I'm part fey, but I know my grandmother can. I've seen her do it," Deena told him.

"So, my father could possibly…?" Josh's question trailed off.

"Not if he's in the fey realm," Deena was quick to reply. "Traveling like that only works within each plane of existence, from

133

what I've gathered. If he's in the fey realm, it would take a whole lot more to bring him here to the mortal realm. It doesn't happen all that often. Travel between the different planes of existence is dangerous, tricky, and really better left to the Mother of All. It takes Her kind of power to do it safely, and as you can imagine, She doesn't do it lightly."

"But what about all those folktales about mortals falling down rabbit holes into faerie?" Josh asked, his eyes dancing with humor in a way that made her heart warm. He was such a special man. A warrior one minute and a gentle lover the next. No wonder she was in love with him.

That thought didn't shock her. She'd known it for a while, but she hadn't quite admitted it to herself. Still, if she was going to choose a man to fall for, Josh was the ideal...even if he did still have a few magical problems to work out. She hoped she could convince him that they needed to work on his magic training for a good *long* while.

"Some of those stories might have a bit of truth to them, but I'd say the majority are just myths. It is said that the Destroyer was trying hard to make gateways to other realms to bring demons across to fight on her behalf, or lay traps for those of other realms who were aligned against her in this one. There's evidence some of her followers have tried to follow in her footsteps. I could see the *Venifucus* laying traps like that, using the fey realm—or perhaps even more dangerous places that they might be able to access. But that's all conjecture on my part. I don't know for sure. I'm kind of isolated here on the farm." She grinned at him and walked out of the ring, stopping to pet Buccaneer, her steadfast horse friend who had carried the two former mages to the stone circle for her.

Deena began walking with the horse at her side, back toward the barn. Several of the other animals had come along, keeping watch from outside the stone circle, and they paraded back to the homestead alongside them, a loose group moving slowly, but with determination.

She walked with them all, directly into the barn, and started putting out extra food and treats for them. They'd been so good to stand between her and danger, she could do no less than thank them for it. She also wanted to check them all over to make certain no one had been injured in the battle.

"I'm going to be a while here," Deena

told Josh as they stood in the wide doorway to the barn. "Why don't you get cleaned up and I can help with your injuries."

He walked right up to her and took her into his arms. Finally. That's what she'd needed. A gentle hug from the man she loved after the hell they'd both been through that day.

He leaned down to kiss her, and she met him halfway, rising on her toes. It was a kiss of welcome and of thanks. A kiss of relief and of respect. Their relationship had taken off in new, unexpected directions. So much had happened, so quickly, it had lifted them beyond the normal progression of dating, kissing, fooling around and so on.

They'd jumped right from their first night together to mortal combat, and that was bound to change perspectives and accelerate the entire process. She didn't mind, but she wasn't sure exactly what he was thinking. Would he back off now? Or would he meet her halfway?

The kiss said, more eloquently than words, that he probably wouldn't be backing away anytime soon. She grasped his shoulders, her senses alight with the promise of him. Of Josh. And what they could be together.

"Ahem." A throat cleared rather deliberately nearby.

They broke apart quickly, Josh taking a ready stance that impressed Deena, while her head was still spinning from the abrupt change. If they were going to have to fight again, it would take her a few minutes to get her act together.

Thankfully, there was no danger. It was just Duncan. He'd returned while they'd been otherwise occupied. She hadn't even noticed the inevitable energy surge when he'd popped back to her farm. Of course, a certain werewolf hottie had been distracting her. Still, she *should* have noticed something like that.

"Darn it," she whispered, stepping forward to meet Duncan. "We've got to get those wards back up. Even you wouldn't have been able to take me by surprise—no matter how distracted I was—if my wards had been in place."

"My fault, Deena," Josh said quickly, stepping up beside her. "I'm sorry."

Was he sorry he'd kissed her? She looked over at him, and his expression said quite the contrary, which mollified her almost-hurt feelings. She saw the blood on his sleeve and touched his shoulder.

"We should patch you up before we do anything else. You're still bleeding," she observed, trying to keep the worry out of her tone.

Josh glanced down at his sleeve. "It's nothing a shift won't cure," he replied off-handedly.

"Good idea," Duncan said, entering the conversation for the first time since his return. "You can scout the perimeter a lot faster in your wolf form than we can on foot. And it will heal your wounds. Two birds, one stone." Duncan looked pleased with the idea. "Meanwhile, I can assist Deena in preparing to raise the wards. Once you come back and give us the all clear, the three of us can work together to install something even stronger than what was here before."

"I thought you were going to question Reggie and Felicia?" Josh asked Duncan rather pointedly.

"I am, but I can't leave you both here with no protections on the farm. Wards first, then questions, then I'll probably return again to discuss a few matters that are still outstanding." His eyes held secrets as he gazed at Josh, but Deena didn't think any topic Duncan had yet to raise would be harmful to either herself or Josh. Duncan was one of the good guys. "Besides," Duncan went on. "Your two attackers will be unconscious for some time to come. They're in a safe place for now, under guard, in case you were wondering."

Josh looked like he might challenge the fey warrior further, but desisted. He walked toward the horse trough and the old-fashioned water pump there, stripping off his shirt as he went.

Deena had seen him naked the night before, of course, but the sight of Josh's lean muscles was still something to behold. He seemed so unaware of his allure, and that was even sexier. He took off his jeans quickly and paused only a moment to bend and run some fresh cold water over his head.

As he straightened and shook out, he was already shifting shape to that of his wolf. He held Deena's gaze as he transformed, and her breath caught at the message in his glowing eyes. He'd known she was watching him, and he'd liked it.

Well, so had she. Josh was, quite possibly,

the sexiest man alive.

CHAPTER TEN

This time, Duncan's throat clearing was more pronounced as she stared after Josh. He was fully wolf and trotting away, his tail up as if he owned the universe. Strutting, she thought. Showing off for his girl—for her. A warm, fuzzy feeling filled her heart, but Duncan was waiting. She turned to the fey mage.

"Now that you've effectively gotten rid of him, what did you want to say to me?" she challenged.

"Am I that transparent?" Duncan's eyes twinkled with amusement, but she wasn't fooled. He'd deliberately gotten her alone so they could talk. He wasn't fooling anybody. Including Josh.

"I will help you with your animal friends as we talk, if that's all right with you. I have a fondness for the critters of this realm," he told her.

"Really?" Somehow, she hadn't pegged Duncan le Fey for an animal lover, but she was happy to be wrong.

He helped her finish scooping out extra feed and treats. Much to her surprise, Duncan was an immediate hit with the citizens of her barn. They liked him and came to him eagerly for nose rubs and pats on the back.

She noticed him watching her out of the corner of his eye, but she didn't call him on it until she was done with her animal friends. When they finished up—a task that took less than five minutes all told, since she'd done most of the work before Duncan had shown up—she faced him squarely.

"What? Do I have soot on my nose?" As she said it, she remembered the nasty smoke Felicia had been throwing and hoped to heaven she didn't have any residue of that gross stuff on her anywhere. Or on her farm.

"No, I was just watching you move to see if any of those singe marks on your clothing signify deeper injuries."

Oh. That was nice of him. She started walking with him, a little thrown by his concern. She hadn't seen him often in recent years, so she wasn't used to his concern. Anyone's concern, really. Aside from her animals. Living alone on the farm had affected her more than she realized.

"No. I'm okay. Nothing a shower and some calendula ointment won't cure," she said as they walked toward the house.

"Well, then." They arrived at the door, and he motioned politely for her precede him into the house. "I saw the way you and Joshua were looking at each other, and the level of power required to defeat those two high-level *Venifucus* mages had to be greater than anything I've observed in either one of you alone."

They were standing in her kitchen, having come in the back door. She wasn't sure she liked being questioned this way in her own home.

"Your point?" she prompted, growing impatient with the whole thing. It had already been a tough day. This was just taking it that one step too far.

Duncan sighed and pulled out one of the kitchen chairs for her. She sat, almost unconsciously. She was *so* tired. She wished he'd just say what he was after so they could get on with things before she collapsed in a heap.

"I just want you to be sure you know what you're getting into with him. I don't want to see you hurt. He's...a bit...wild for you, Deena." Duncan looked somewhat uncomfortable with his own words.

As well he should be! How dare he disparage Josh?

"All I'm saying is, are you sure your grandmother would approve?" Duncan asked.

The crafty old bugger. She got the feeling he'd been trying to provoke her, but that last bit about her grandmother...

"You know as well as I do that Grandmother would be pleased to see me involved with a shifter. The fact that he's got a lot of fey blood in him is probably a bonus. But the most important thing is that he's the right man for me. And I won't say anything more on the subject to you right now. It's only fair that any declarations I have to make be made to Josh first, not to you."

Duncan regarded her steadily for a long moment, then slapped one hand down on the kitchen table as he smiled. She almost jumped at the sound, but Duncan was still smiling.

"As I thought. I just had to say it, Deena. Forgive me for being an old busybody, but I do like your grandmother—and you—and I don't want to see you hurt in any way."

"Josh would never hurt me," she said, knowing in her heart the truth of her words.

With that out of the way, they started discussing the best way to go about reconstructing her wards. They wouldn't be the same. No, the plan was to make them better than they had been before. Stronger and constructed of more flavors of energy, utilizing all three of their brands of magic. The very fact that Duncan was including Josh in his calculations was significant, and appeased the sense of outrage she'd had a few moments before when Duncan had called Josh wild and questioned their involvement.

When Josh walked in a few minutes later, he was dressed again in his T-shirt and jeans and his hair was slicked back. He must've dunked his head under the water spigot again. She couldn't blame him. It had been a hell of a day so far, and it wasn't over yet.

She could do with a reviving splash of water herself.

She went to the sink and grabbed a clean dishtowel, wetting it down and using it to rub at her face. Within moments, she felt a little more awake and alert. Good. She'd need that for the magic they were about to do next.

"There's a rental car parked up near your mailbox," Josh told her. "From the scent, I'd say it was Felicia's ride. I followed her trail down from the car. She must've ditched the rental up there by the road and come in on foot while we were distracted with Reggie."

"I figured it had to be something like that," Deena replied. "How do we get rid of her car?"

"I'll handle it," Duncan told them. "I can drop it at an airport in the next state and make it look as if Felicia returned it herself. As for the dirt bike I saw out by the barn…"

"I'd like to hang onto it if it's clear of Reggie's magic and won't bring down more trouble on our heads," Josh replied before Deena could answer.

"Any magic either of your attackers had left when their energies were reclaimed by the Mother of All have dissipated by now, but I'll check the bike over in detail before I leave. Then, of course, there are mundane ways to alter serial numbers—" Duncan started to say, but Josh cut him off with a friendly wave of his hand.

"I know how to make it untraceable by human standards," Josh revealed. "I was just concerned about some kind of magical trace."

Duncan nodded slowly. "Well, as I said, I'll check, but I think it's probably clean now that Reginald's magic has been permanently removed."

Josh nodded with apparent satisfaction. Deena wasn't sure what he wanted the bike for, but living frugally as she did, it seemed a shame to toss it. They couldn't very well return it to Reggie's next of kin, so the only other alternative—throwing it away—seemed too wasteful.

Plus, she had to consider that Josh had been dropped off on her doorstep with no means of transportation. Maybe he felt trapped on the farm with no wheels. She didn't think that was the case, but she also knew that grown men usually liked to have some independent method of transportation at their disposal. And motorcycles of any kind were probably the ultimate guy toy.

While it was true that Josh could always go wolf and cover a lot of distance on his own four paws, that wasn't the most practical means of getting around. For one thing, he'd be naked when he shifted back to human form. Of course, she didn't mind seeing him naked, and he didn't seem to have the same inhibitions as most other beings. Still, a fellow could get arrested by human cops for being naked in the middle of town.

"Planning your getaway already?" Duncan challenged Josh's motive for keeping the bike in a way Deena never would have.

"Nothing of the sort," Josh answered in a firm voice. "It's just always good to take advantage of opportunities, and having a new vehicle on the farm that's able to handle cross-country terrain seems like a good one. I've taken a look at Deena's truck and that thing is lucky it's still running. It could never handle even a mile on grass in its current state and the bike gives us flexibility if we ever need to make a run for it."

Deena's heart melted a little bit more. He'd been thinking of her safety. That's why he wanted the bike. As a means of escape, should they ever need it. He was taking care of her again, and it made her want to reach out and kiss him breathless. If Duncan hadn't been standing there, she would have done just that. As it was…they still had work to do and a fey warrior all but tapping his foot in impatience to get on with it.

Duncan nodded at Josh's explanation and let the subject drop.

"Normally, I'd wait to raise wards until you were rested and at peak strength, but this cannot wait, and with three of us working the spells, we should be able to do something worthwhile…and hard to break," Duncan said, eyeing her with a concerned expression.

"Three of us?" Josh repeated. "You know I'm just a novice when it comes to magic, Duncan."

"A novice couldn't have done what you just did to a *Venifucus* mage," Duncan countered. "You may not know all the methods and spells yet, but you'll get there. What counts, when all is said and done, is power and intent. You've got those in spades."

"Glad you think so," Josh muttered, just at audible level.

She wanted to go to him, but Duncan's presence inhibited her. Josh didn't seem to be inhibited, though. He walked right up to her at the kitchen sink and took the damp towel out of her hands. Invading her personal space in a way she rather liked, he took over dabbing at her face, which made her think maybe there were smudges of dirt or smoke that she hadn't known about.

But when he followed up the gentle cleansing with a kiss to her forehead and a loose embrace, she wanted nothing more than to melt into him and stay there forever. This tender side of Josh was dangerously attractive, and somewhat surprising.

"We'd better get started," Duncan said in a voice that was just a little too loud as he rose from his chair at the kitchen table. "I have places to go and people to question, and I suspect you two need to rest and recover a bit, which you can't do until the wards are back up and your territory is better protected."

Josh nodded and stepped back. Deena was sad to lose his comforting warmth, but she agreed with Duncan. They had to get those wards up and running before she could rest easy in her own home.

Josh was fascinated by the spells Duncan taught him and the creation of the wards around Deena's farm. Thankfully, the skill seemed to come easily to him, and Duncan was a great teacher. Deena followed Duncan's lead, too, which surprised Josh at first, but then again, he figured one person couldn't be expert on all aspects of magic. Plus, Duncan was one hundred percent fey and very, very old, though he didn't look it. He'd probably forgotten more about magic and spells than Josh or Deena would ever know.

It took a couple of hours, and by the time Duncan pronounced himself satisfied with the layers of protection they'd erected around the farm, Josh was dragging. Deena looked tired, too, and Josh put his arm around her waist to support her as they turned to walk back to the house.

Setting the wards had involved walking the perimeter of the farm, with a long stop in the stone circle. Each time they stopped to layer a spell, the magic poured out of him— and Deena—and he could almost feel it sinking into the land. It felt good and pure, but there was also no question, it drained him.

Duncan had looked at him a little oddly the first time they called the magic and those pure white sparks appeared. As near as Josh could figure, Deena and he were somehow tuned to work together now, and when they added their magic to the mix, it came out unified, with that white light show he'd seen first in the circle of stones during the full moon ritual.

It had grown stronger since then, which was a little disconcerting, but Josh figured it was a good thing. The more power to keep their enemies at bay, the better.

Duncan left soon after, and Josh was glad. He wanted nothing more than to collapse in a bed and not think about magic or bad guys or anything other than holding Deena in his arms.

"I'm glad that's done," Deena said as they walked through the house, heading for the guest room by unspoken agreement. "I'm going to shower, then I want sleep."

"I hear you," Josh agreed. "You take the shower first," he offered as they stepped into the generous-sized guest room.

He was glad of his habitual neatness because he'd changed the sheets and made the bed before starting breakfast that morning—which reminded him. They'd never gotten to eat. She must've cleared the kitchen of their uneaten breakfast while he was out scouting the perimeter in his wolf form, and they'd been so busy since, there hadn't been time to do much more than gulp down water and eat a few crackers she'd had in her jacket pocket.

While Deena showered, Josh set up a moveable feast. He set up trays with thick homemade bread, creamy farm-fresh cheese, fruit from the trees out back, and a variety of beverages, with ice in tumblers, and brought them into the guest room, placing them on the small table by the window.

He'd planned to join Deena in the shower. For one thing, he'd wanted to be sure she didn't have any serious injuries that she'd been hiding all this time. For another, he'd wanted to hold her body close and maybe convince her that sleep was overrated. But she was out of the shower before he could make a move toward the bathroom door.

The smile that lit her face when she saw the food trays was his reward, though. Wrapped in a soft terrycloth robe that had been hanging on the back of the bathroom door for her guests, she made a beeline for the table and had barely sat down before she started eating.

Satisfaction filled him. The wolf rumbled happily in his heart. It liked providing for its mate.

CHAPTER ELEVEN

After eating, they tumbled into bed and slept the sleep of the just. It wasn't even early evening when they fell asleep, needing rest after the physical and magical exertions of the morning and afternoon, so Deena wasn't surprised when she woke up to find the moon just rising in the sky. She could see it out the window of the guest room, and it painted the dark room in its stark white light.

She looked over at the face of her sleeping lover. Josh. He really was the most handsome man she'd ever known, but more than that, he had a beautiful soul. She hadn't known him long as mortals counted time—which was how she imagined her fey grandmother would phrase it—but she knew him better than any man she'd ever been with. Not that there'd been that many. And none since she'd moved way out here. But she knew Josh's soul. She'd shared magic with him. She knew the flavor and tenor of his innermost being, and even better, she'd really liked what she'd found there.

No. *Like* was too simple a word. She was astounded by the depth of the man. He was complex and earthy in a way that stole her breath. His wildness was part of his very nature, but it wasn't dangerous—at least not to her. He had a sense of honor as strong as the day was long, and his soul craved justice for those who had been wronged. He lived by his own code, and it was a strict one. An ancient one. One few men could live up to, but Josh managed, even in this more decadent day and age of man.

One didn't simply *like* a man like that. No. This was a man she could love. A man she *did* love.

"Penny for your thoughts." Josh's voice was a deep whisper in the dark with a hint of sexy growl.

"I was thinking how much I admire you," she told him, brushing back the hair that had fallen across his brow with one hand, a gentle caress on his skin. She was taking a chance, but she thought she knew his heart, and she hoped—she prayed—he was thinking along the same lines as her.

"That's good," he said, rising on one elbow to look down at her, lying at his side. "Because I admire the hell out of you, too, Deena." He punctuated his words with a kiss. "In fact, I actually…"

He paused, and she held her breath.

"The thing is… I actually…love you. I hope it's not too soon to say that." His expression spoke of his uncertainty and concern that he might be rushing her, but she felt the smile leap to her lips as she all but tackled him.

She kissed him with all the pent-up joy in her heart, pushing him down to the bed so that she was on top. She was the aggressor for the time being. She was letting him know in the most basic way possible that he hadn't been wrong to take that chance and speak his heart to her.

When she let him up for air, she was gasping for breath but still grinning like a fool.

"I take it you're okay with what I just said?" he asked, one eyebrow raised devilishly.

"More than okay," she said between breaths. "I love you, too, Josh. You're the best man I've ever known, in every way that counts."

He looked a little uncomfortable with that last bit, but she wouldn't take it back. He was hers now. She was staking a claim. He might not realize it yet, but she'd do everything in her power to make sure this worked out. That *they* worked out.

There wasn't time for more words then as Josh turned the tables, moving so that she was under him, and he was kissing her breathless once again. He really was a good kisser. Scratch that. He was a *great* kisser. And everything else he did to her was pretty darn awesome too.

He wasn't one of those men who needed a map and a compass to figure out what a woman liked. No. He *knew*. The sexy so-and-so.

She got a little angry when she thought about the women he must've known in the past to gain such knowledge, but whether he realized it or not, he was well on his way to becoming a one-woman man. Deena didn't have any plans to let him go any time soon.

Come to think of it, she didn't really want to contemplate *ever* letting him go.

She'd fallen asleep in the damp terrycloth robe, though by the time they'd finished eating, it had mostly dried. Josh had worn only a pair of shorts, so all the luscious, warm muscles of his chest and arms were available for her to caress. Mmm. He was perfect. Perfect for her.

She stroked his arms as he untied the simple knot at her waist. He continued his drugging kisses as he peeled the robe open, side-to-side, revealing her naked body.

Soon, his kisses trailed down over her jawbone, eliciting a moan of delight as he worked his way downward, pausing at her breasts. His hands were busy, too, moving her thighs apart to make room, and then delving between, touching her most intimate places and preparing the way for an even more intimate invasion that she was eager to experience again. And again. And again.

But she didn't want to be just along for the ride this time. No, she had something else in mind.

Pushing at his muscular shoulders, she got him to move back. He rolled with her until she was on top. *There. That was better.*

She straddled him, happy to discover that he'd removed his shorts somewhere along the way. There was nothing between them but the open bathrobe. She leaned up and removed it, sliding it off one shoulder at a time, holding his gaze.

Deena laughed as she flung it across the room, feeling freer to be herself than she ever had. Josh made everything fun and exciting. He was so good for her. He brought her out of her shell without even trying and dared her to try new things.

Speaking of which... She leaned down and kissed him. She reluctantly left his mouth, kissing her way down his hard body, teasing and caressing as she went along. When she grasped him in her hand, he shuddered with pleasure, and she felt a little zing of triumph. She'd done that to him— and she planned to do a lot more before she was through with him.

By the time she licked the tip of his hardness and took him into her mouth, he was growling a deep, sexy murmur of sound that made her body respond. She was so ready for him, it wasn't even funny, but she was enjoying learning the intimate taste of him and the feel of him against her tongue.

Josh had other ideas, though. She must've been doing something a little too right because his growl deepened, and a moment later, he lifted her bodily away from him, flipped her over, positioning her on her hands and knees, and entered her from behind. He was urgent, but cautious, letting her take him in small increments until she comfortable with the invasion. He was a big man, and she was glad he'd taken his time at first, but now…she wanted motion.

Hard, fast, deep motion.

His growls were answered by her moans of pleasure as Josh hit a little spot within her on each stroke that sent her pleasure skyrocketing to the moon and back. As the sensations intensified, she began to shake, but he supported her, one of his big hands holding her hip, the other supporting her abdomen. He surrounded her until she wasn't sure where she ended and he began. She felt so at one with him, it was almost sacred.

And then…at long last…he joined her on that rocket to the moon, making the journey last while he held her and filled her, cherished her and whispered words of love that were engraved, at that moment, indelibly on her heart. She was with him through it all, and she would remember this moment for as long as she lived. One perfect, blissful moment with the only man she had ever truly loved.

CHAPTER TWELVE

The next morning started out a bit like the previous one, but after Josh woke alone, cleaned up and made breakfast for Deena, they actually got to eat it this time. They spent a bit longer at the table than strictly necessary, but Josh liked the sort of goofy way Deena was looking at him. He liked teasing her too. She responded to him so beautifully it was hard not to make love to her right there on the kitchen table.

He was contemplating how to go about it when Deena straightened, and Josh felt the influx of familiar magic a moment later. Duncan was back. The wards were functioning, alerting them both to the fey man's arrival, but they didn't keep Duncan out. He'd helped build them, so he was one of the few who would always be allowed in.

Though Josh's plans for seduction were foiled by Duncan's arrival, Josh was curious to find out if Duncan had learned anything from Reggie and Felicia. Josh followed Deena to the front door, where Duncan was waiting politely on the front steps.

"Come in," Deena invited after she'd opened the door. Duncan inclined his head in greeting as Josh nodded, just once, at him. "We're just finishing breakfast. Can I offer you anything?" Deena led the way back into the kitchen.

"Just some coffee, if you have it," Duncan replied, following her. Josh brought up the rear, after securing the front door, keeping an eye on Duncan and Deena as they moved through the house.

"I think that can be arranged," Deena said as they entered the big kitchen.

She went straight to the coffee pot and poured a fresh cup for Duncan. She then refreshed Josh's cup before her own and set the pot back on the warmer. Duncan sat comfortably at the table, seeming to savor the first sip of Deena's excellent dark roast.

After a moment, he set the cup down and

looked at them both, his expression serious. "I wanted to let you know what I've discovered so far from your attackers. They came here specifically for you, Deena." He let that sit for a moment before continuing. "They definitely are members of the *Venifucus* order, and they report to another mage who is even higher up in the organization. I'm still working to get information on him, and more about the order in general, but the really bad part is that they knew all about you, Deena. Reginald had been specifically tasked to watch for your power, and apparently, he'd noted a flare of it the night before last. He figured between himself and Felicia, who he called in at the last minute, they'd be more than a match for you. They hadn't bargained on your abilities, Josh, so that was a break for us."

"There wouldn't have been a flare of magic if not for me, though, so I'm really to blame for all of this," Josh admitted, putting it out in the open. The attack had been his fault, at its core. Reggie wouldn't have spotted Deena if Josh hadn't been there... If they hadn't made love and caused the power surge that brought her to Reggie's attention.

Deena reached out and covered his hand with hers on the tabletop. What a soft thing she was, both physically and emotionally. Deena was the beating heart of him, and she made him a better man. That she would so easily forgive him bringing her to the attention of their enemies—even inadvertently—meant a more than he could say.

"Believe me," Duncan said to him, "sooner or later, something would have happened, and they would have found her. Much better that you were here to do what you did. The two of you, working together, were able to defeat Reginald and Felicia, which is a feather in both of your caps. They weren't just simple foot soldiers. They were highly-placed *Venifucus* mages. It's a coup that you were able to defeat them, and a good result for our side. So, well done."

Duncan took a sip of his coffee and went on. "They realized a bit too late who you were, Josh. Reginald was highly-placed enough to have heard about the rogue wolf-mage—which is what he called you—that some of the lesser mages had been hunting. It sounds like they lost your trail and didn't know you'd be here."

"Son of a…" Josh muttered. He'd hoped the enemies he'd had to fight on his way to this place had just been random opportunistic magic users. To learn he'd truly been hunted made him really mad, and it infuriated his inner wolf. He wasn't *prey*!

"If they'd realized sooner who you are, and that you were here, they would've come with a posse to capture you both. As it was, I think we caught a few breaks here, for which we should be very grateful."

"Oh, I am," Deena said at once. "The Mother of All has been watching all of this much more closely than usual. She even appeared to Josh, which was unexpected."

Duncan looked at her, then at Josh and turned the conversation on end with two simple words.

"I know."

Deena frowned, and Josh sensed a change in the air. "How could you know that?" Deena finally asked. "We didn't tell anyone. Josh, did you tell Duncan?"

"Nope," Josh answered her, eyeing Duncan with interest. He definitely had the air of someone who was about to reveal something that might just be life-altering.

"She said you would be tested, did She

not?" Duncan asked. Slowly, Josh nodded. "Facing those mages was part of your test, but merging your magic with Deena's was the really telling part. As a priestess, Deena has sworn her life to the Goddess. The Mother of All saw into your heart through Her connection with Deena, and found your soul to be pure."

"How—?" Deena started to ask, but Duncan raised one hand to cut off her question.

"Because you passed the many tests laid before you, Josh, I am empowered to discuss a greater opportunity for you to serve the Mother of All...if you want to."

Josh was intrigued. "Tell me more."

Deena had long suspected there had to be more to Duncan than met the eye. For one thing, it was unusual for a fey to stay so long in the mortal realm without some greater purpose to fulfill. Deena's grandmother had been here for centuries, but she was a priestess of the Lady, a servant of the Mother of All. It was the will of the Goddess that kept Deena's grandmother here, doing the Goddess's work and helping those who served Her.

Duncan hadn't seemed to have the same kind of ties. Though Deena knew all about how he had come into the mortal realm almost accidentally when a powerful young priestess had inadvertently opened the portal to bring him through, Deena had no idea what he'd been doing—other than house sitting and watching over an old vampire friend.

This was the first indication that there might be some higher purpose to his presence. If Duncan was aware of what had happened between Josh and the Lady, then Duncan, too, had to have a strong connection with Her. She had to have spoken to him directly. Somehow.

What was he that he spoke to the Goddess without the intervention of a priestess?

"Have you ever heard of a *Chevalier de la Lumiere*? Literally translated, it means a Knight of the Light." Duncan looked down, taking a breath, then looked up again, pinning Josh with a suddenly intense gaze. Bright golden light shone out of his eyes and began to surround his entire body. "I am one. As is your sire."

"My father?" Josh asked, seemingly dazed

by the transformation happening before their eyes.

Where Duncan had sat, in plain modern clothing, the light enveloping him revealed something very different. The golden glow showed a man in armor of pure energy, arcane symbols lighting his breastplate and gauntlets.

Duncan stood, and Deena could see the sword of light forming at his side. It was like a visual overlay. Underneath the glowing armor was still the man who had entered her kitchen, still wearing the dark pants and shirt in which Duncan had arrived. Over that, now, was an encasing golden light of pure magical energy. Goddess touched, Deena could tell.

Josh stood, too, facing Duncan from across the big farm kitchen.

"Yes, Josh. Your father is a brother to me in the sacred Order that serves the Lady. He is a Knight of the Light, but like me, he has been trapped in the fey realm for a very long time. I was able to break through the barrier evil had placed around me when a new and powerful priestess unwittingly called for my aid. Since then, I have been here, in the mortal realm, where I can actually do some good in the fight against evil. Your father still needs rescue, and I believe it is something you can accomplish—you and Deena together—with your joined, amplified power."

"Why can't the Goddess just bust him out?" Josh asked. It was a rather irreverent question, but Deena had been wondering the same thing.

Duncan shook his head. "She is all powerful—within certain constraints. Her influence in this realm is much greater, for example, than in those realms which are still clouded by strong magic. Faerie is practically built from magic alone, and those with evil intent—like Elspeth and her followers—have made the most of that over the centuries." Duncan sighed.

"So, my father was trapped? That's why he abandoned my mother?" Josh asked, his voice sounding strange to Deena's ears, as if he was trying very hard to control his emotions.

Duncan nodded. "He loved her. He still loves her. She was his mate, in the truest sense of the word. It broke his heart when he realized he couldn't come back to this realm."

Josh was overly calm. Deena wanted to go to him. She stood, but she found she couldn't go far because she started to feel funny.

She recognized the feeling, though, and didn't worry. She gave herself up to the sensation and knew that Duncan and Josh would be speaking with a much higher authority at any moment.

Josh felt something happening with Deena through their new connection and turned just in time to see her eyes change. Deena was somewhere else, and in her place, the Goddess had come to call. Again.

"Rest easy, young Joshua," the Goddess said through Deena. "All is well, and you have passed the many tests placed before you these past few months. You never once wavered toward evil, and you have shown yourself to have a pure and giving heart. We have watched over you for a long time, Joshua, and We would have you as one of Our Knights, if you are willing."

Josh was floored by the offer. The Goddess was singling him out as something special? Him? The lone wolf who had no friends and no ties...

But he was tied irrevocably to Deena now. Maybe it was time to start forging some other bonds. Who better to serve than the Lady, Herself?

Josh had never been overly religious in an outward way, but his faith in the Goddess had seen him through tough times more than once. He had always striven to be the kind of man his mother would be proud of, and his mother was a deeply devout woman, filled with faith, even in the darkest times.

Josh sank to one knee before the Goddess in Deena's form.

"Milady, I have always sought to live my life in service to Your Light."

The Goddess smiled, and Josh felt the warmth of her radiance.

"We have seen that truth in your actions. You need to know that those of fey blood must choose to serve Us. We cannot command those of the immortal realms the way We can those of the mortal realm. You are a child of both places, Joshua, so it is your decision...as it was Deena's...and her grandmother's...and Duncan's...and your father's. We fear dark times are ahead of all beings of the Light, and We seek your alliance and service to help combat the evil that will come against you. Will you serve the Light as a *Chevalier?*"

Josh looked up at the Goddess, sure of his decision even before she asked.

"I will, Milady. It will be my honor." Josh bowed his head and felt a magical benediction rain down around him.

The Goddess's blessing energized him and brought him something...more. Something he didn't quite understand yet, but he assumed he'd have to learn how to master before he could truly serve Her.

"Good. Then, rise, *Sir* Joshua, and be clad in the Light."

Josh got to his feet, an aura of power gathering around him. Though he couldn't see all of himself, he was aware of the shield of light that formed around his legs and arms. Unlike Duncan's golden armor, Josh's was the pure white he had seen the few times his magic had risen with Deena's. White sparkles surrounded him, coalescing into a kind of energy shield that surrounded his body, following its contours faithfully.

"Duncan will be your first teacher, but We want you and Deena to work on something special. And thus, We set you your first task in Our name," the Lady told

174

him. "We wish you to open the barrier between this realm and faerie, just enough to pull your sire through. He has been trapped long enough and has missed too much of your life. He is also more familiar with your particular brand of energy and will be better able to teach you how to master it."

"I'll do my best, Milady," Josh replied, feeling a bit lost because he didn't even know where to start to try to do something like that. He hoped Deena had a clue. Or maybe Duncan.

"We leave you now, Our newest Knight. Welcome to the Order, and Our deepest thanks for choosing to serve the Light. We will need your strength in the battles to come." The Goddess left Deena, and as before, Deena swayed, and Josh caught her.

He placed her on her chair, crouching beside her while he monitored her return to her own body. He held one of her hands and stroked her cheek with his free hand.

When she opened her eyes, the first thing she saw was him. Her eyes widened.

"Josh, you're glowing!"

"Very sparkly, indeed," Duncan agreed with a grin. "But perhaps we should tone down the armor for now. Follow my lead," the fey warrior said, doing something with his magic that Josh could just about follow after the days spent observing and practicing with Deena.

When the glow had receded, Josh realized the barrier around his body was still there, just not visible. That would be handy if he kept getting attacked by mages. Of course, he'd just agreed to be a Knight. Chances were, battle would be in his future more than not.

His inner wolf wanted to bat at the encasing energy at first, but once he got used to it and realized its protective properties, he made peace with it. The wolf seemed to recognize the flavor of the energy with its enhanced senses, and Josh understood that the protection was of the Goddess, but also part of his own energies…and Deena's. The wolf rumbled with happiness. Already, he was joining more closely with his mate. The wolf liked that. A lot.

"What happened?" Deena asked, sitting up straighter as she recovered.

"Well, you know the Goddess came through you again, right?" Josh started, not really sure how to break the news of his elevation to knighthood to her.

"Yeah, I felt what was about to happen. What did She say?"

Josh was still at a loss for words. Duncan cleared his throat, and both Josh and Deena looked over at him.

"The Lady saw fit to ask Josh to join Her elite warriors and pledge to train as a *Chevalier*, like myself and his sire." Duncan bowed his head briefly.

"Really? So, did you do it?" Deena wanted to know, looking back at Josh. "Of course you did," she answered her own question. "Oh, Josh! I knew you were even more special than I first thought." She reached out to him, throwing her arms around his neck. He moved closer so she wouldn't topple off the chair, hugging her close.

"You're not mad I didn't consult you about my decision first?" he asked quietly, needing to know, despite Duncan's presence.

"Not at all," she answered just as quietly. "You know my heart."

His breath caught at her intimate words. "You're right," he answered. "And you know mine. I love you, Deena. More than anything or anyone."

He kissed her softly, just a quick peck to

solidify his words. Duncan was still there, but this needed to be said right now, before more time passed. So much had happened in such a short time. Emotions were running high and needed to be acknowledged.

When they moved apart, Deena looked into Josh's eyes. "I love you too."

"That's good, because it's a little more...complicated for shifters than I've probably led you to believe. When we fall in love, it's a lifelong thing. It's a *mating* thing. Deena. Mating is for keeps." He took a breath for courage. "Will you be my mate?"

Joy lit her face before she breathed the word that completed his world.

"Yes."

EPILOGUE

"I'm sorry I couldn't come back to visit the calf until today," Grace said in her sweet, high voice as she stroked the calf's nose. Josh was standing in the doorway to the barn watching Deena and their young visitor. "Mama said you had visitors and I wasn't to interrupt, but when my brother saw that the car by your mailbox was gone this morning, Mama said it would be okay to come over for a little while. She said to ask about your houseguest, though." Grace's small face scrunched up with puzzlement. "Is he a relation?"

Deena chuckled and glanced back toward Josh. She'd known when he'd arrived, but apparently Grace hadn't. He walked closer and took Deena's hand in his very deliberately. He noted Grace's start of surprise when he appeared and her inquisitive expression when Josh took Deena's hand.

Josh was glad they'd never really explained who he was supposed to be in relation to Deena, because the cousin story would never work. And it would've made things awkward now. As it was, Deena's neighbors would probably be a little shocked by the suddenness of his appearance on the scene, but that couldn't be helped.

"Josh is my husband," Deena replied, before he could say anything. His inner wolf wanted to howl his happiness. This was the first time Deena had claimed him as her mate in front of witnesses.

Sure, Duncan probably knew they were mates, but the actual words had remained pretty much unspoken for the most part. This declaration was something fresh and shiny. A set of words that meant something spectacular because of the context.

Grace might only be one little girl, but it was clear that Deena's warnings about the Amish grapevine were spot on. They'd been keeping an eye on her house and knew when there was a vehicle that didn't belong. While it was reassuring in a way that Deena had such interested neighbors, it didn't do much for Josh's peace of mind that nobody had come over to see if she was okay. In fact, they'd stayed away while her *visitors* were present. If Deena had been all alone, or in real trouble, how long would it have been before someone checked on her? Josh didn't like to think of the answer to that question.

"You got married?" Grace asked, her voice rising impossibly higher in excitement. She was smiling, which Josh took as a good sign, but he wondered what the older members of the neighborhood would think of this rather hasty event.

Deena was smiling too, and it helped settle Josh's concerns. She knew her neighbors better than he did. Hopefully she'd figure out a way to make this all sound reasonable so that she could continue to enjoy a good relationship with the folk in the area.

"It had been planned for a while," Deena said, skirting around the truth with ease, but Josh would back her up no matter what story she concocted. He planned to be a good mate. He'd stand with his woman, even if she told people he was an alien from another planet.

Hopefully, it wouldn't come to that.

"Our families were involved," Deena went on making stuff up that seemed to satisfy the young girl. He wondered if Grace's mother would be as easily fooled. "We were just waiting for Josh to be able to move here and the visitors came to help us do the paperwork and make our union legal in the eyes of man, and in the presence of the Almighty."

Josh had noticed before the way Deena couched her belief in the Divine in terms that wouldn't upset her conservative neighbors. Only Josh knew that when Deena referred to the Almighty, she was thinking of the benevolent Goddess and not the rather strict interpretation of divinity that ruled Grace's family.

He wondered how Deena squared it all in her mind. He knew tolerance was a big part of being a priestess, and Deena's heart was as big as the world. She would never turn away an animal in pain or a little girl who came from a family that had vastly different views on religion.

"Was that your bishop's car?" Grace

asked. "Did he perform the ceremony?"

"It doesn't work quite that way in our sect," Deena said with a kind smile. Josh noticed she didn't go into detail about how that car had belonged to an evil sorceress intent on killing them both. That probably wouldn't go down well on the neighboring farm.

"Are you going to grow a beard now, Mr. Joshua?" Grace asked him. Josh had to laugh. He knew that was something the Amish did, but he just couldn't see himself with a long, scraggly, grandpappy beard.

"Maybe a small one," he allowed, not wanting to burst the little girl's bubble. She probably already knew that her parents' way of life was a bit different from other people's, but far be it from him to make things worse.

"Did you have a big party?" Grace asked Deena as she walked out of the stall patting the calf one last time.

"Not yet. Josh's mother is coming to visit in a few weeks and we'll hold our celebration then. It won't be as big as your sister's wedding last year, though," Deena explained.

"Where is your family, Mr. Joshua?" Grace asked, walking beside him as the three of them walked out of the barn. Sure enough, Mergatroid the pony was eager to get going, as usual, and came right up to Deena for a cuddle.

"My mother is in North Dakota," Josh answered, seeing no harm in answering the child's question, though he couldn't give her an answer about his father. At least not one that would make any sense to her.

"That's very far away, isn't it?" Grace asked, her little voice sounding sad. She asked a whole bunch more questions while she got Mergatroid hitched, and then they were off.

"The news will be all over this valley by nightfall," Deena mused, leaning back against his chest as they both watched Grace and her pony take off down the track between the fields.

Josh put his arms around her and pulled her closer. "You called me your husband."

"Hmm. I did, didn't I?"

He squeezed her as she chuckled. He loved playing with his mate. That she felt comfortable enough to tease him made his inner wolf want to play like a puppy. With her. Only with her.

To all others, his wolf was still a badass

biting machine, but for Deena, he was a fluffy puppy. The woman had changed him forevermore. There was just one thing…

"Who officiates at a priestess's wedding?" he asked, curious. They were mates in the eyes of the Mother of All, but the human parts of them both probably would enjoy having an official ceremony and maybe a party to mark the occasion.

"Another priestess," she murmured, turning in his arms. "Funny you should mention that. After you spoke to your mother this morning and went out to *check the perimeter*—which I think means that you just wanted to go wolf and chase bunnies through our fields—I called my grandmother. She's going to give us a few days with your mother when she visits in December and then my grandmother's going to pop in. She wants to meet both you and your mother. And I sort of asked her if she would…uh…officiate for us. How do you feel about a proper mating ceremony on the Winter Solstice?"

"Seriously?" He liked that she sounded as eager to make their mating official—in front of their families—as he was. He was grinning so hard, his face almost hurt. "I'd love that.

Are you sure you want to wait that long, though? The solstice is still quite a few weeks off."

She punched his shoulder playfully. "I need all the time I can get to find the right dress! And arrange the food and clean the house. There are a million things to do. I want to make a good impression on your mother."

"She's going to love you," he told her, hugging her close and placing biting kisses on her neck. Then a thought occurred to him. "What about your grandmother? Is she up to the trip? Should we go to her? I don't want to put her out. I'm happy to accommodate an elderly lady, and wouldn't want to cause her any trouble."

Deena's gaze went serious as she placed both palms on his shoulders and looked into his eyes. "Never. Ever. Let her hear you call her elderly. She might be my grandmother, but she's fey, Josh. She looks younger than I do. And she outranks me to a huge degree. I think I mentioned...she's the High Priestess. Have you ever heard of Bettina?"

The penny dropped as the name finally connected in Josh's mind. Every shifter had heard of the highly magical woman who served at the right hands of the Lords of all werecreatures.

"Your grandmother is *that* Bettina? *The* High Priestess?"

Josh felt suddenly light headed. If he'd thought his mate was a formidable power, the High Priestess was said to be a force of nature itself.

"It's okay," Deena told him. "She's not as scary as all that. Especially not to you. Not now that you're a Knight."

"Knight in training," he reminded her. He hadn't really come to accept the new title yet. He'd have to learn a lot more before he'd feel truly comfortable presenting himself as a Knight. Especially with the High Priestess Bettina.

Josh wondered if even the magical armor he'd been practicing with would protect him from a wrathful High Priestess should he somehow do something to hurt his mate's feelings. Bettina was said to eat bad shifters for breakfast and snack on evil mages. What kind of family had he gotten himself into?

"I'll call my parents later today, and they'll spread the word to my aunts and uncles, and cousins. I just wanted to make sure the plan was acceptable to you first, before I went ahead and started inviting people. It won't be the size of an Amish wedding, but my side of the family will fill up the house, and then some." Deena was smiling again, probably thinking about seeing her family again. Then she refocused on his stunned face and frowned. "You don't mind, do you?"

"Mind?" He was still trying to come to terms with the idea that Deena had a large extended family he hadn't even considered.

"I kind of want to show you off," she admitted in a shy tone, smiling in that way that made his heart melt.

That was the tipping point. Her happiness was his goal now, and if a big wedding was what she wanted, with all her relations in attendance, that's what he'd give her. He'd do anything for her.

Josh bent to kiss her, pausing only to whisper against her lips, "I love you, Deena. Whatever you want is fine by me."

Anything else she might've said went into the kiss, and they stayed there, locked together in their own private little world of love, surrounded by Deena's misfit animals, who seemed to be watching with approval. Josh might be a predator at heart, but all the creatures on that farm were now under his protection. His and Deena's.

They were a team now and with a little luck, and a whole lot of love, they'd have many decades together to perfect their magic…and their mating.

# # #

EXCERPT:
SNOW MAGIC
A Were-Fey Love Story 2

CHAPTER ONE

North Dakota

Snow was howling as the female wolf padded across the frozen landscape toward her den. It was a lonely den now, and had been that way ever since her pup—the only one she would ever bear—had left on his own quest for truth. She'd known he couldn't stay forever. Just as his sire hadn't been able to stay for very long, but oh, how she had enjoyed the short time she'd had with her mate.

He'd simply gone out one day and had never come back. That had been more than twenty years ago now, but she'd had her pup, beautiful Joshua, who had grown into a powerful young man, to keep her company. At first, she'd been the protector, but as he grew, the roles had reversed and he'd been the one to set her up in this fancy, more secure den on the edge of town, backing onto the wilderness that called to her wild nature.

Evie McCann had been young, even by shifter standards, when she'd met her mate. He hadn't been one of her people, but a man of intense magic from another realm. Faerie. That's what they called his place in the universe, but she'd just thought of him as *hers*.

They'd had only a few short months together before he'd disappeared, and he'd never seen his son. Evie's heart had broken at the loss of her mate and if not for Joshua, she probably wouldn't have made it, but the little boy had his father's magic in his soul and the wild heart of the wolf that had sustained her. They'd lived rough, but they'd made it. Both of them.

And now her son had found a mate of his own.

He'd suffered a crisis earlier in the year when unexpected magic had made him a target for evil. He'd made sure Evie was set up in a secure location before he'd gone into the wild, leading trouble away from her. It had been one of the hardest things she'd ever done—parting with her son—but there had been no other way. She was only a shifter, of low rank in the Pack that she'd left all those years ago to be with her fey mate. She wasn't strong enough to face the kind of danger that was hunting her son, much as it pained her to admit it.

She'd had to let go. The months since had been hard. She'd shifted to her furry form more and more, trying to escape her loneliness, but it didn't really help. She was very much afraid that one day, she'd go out into the wilds and just...never come back. Never reclaim her human form. Her human life.

It was a possibility that she still feared, which she guessed was a healthy attitude. When she got around to embracing the idea, then she'd know she was really in trouble.

Things had turned around a bit recently though. Her son had defeated those who had been hunting him and then mated with a lovely young woman who owned a farm in the Amish country of Pennsylvania. While it was a long distance from the rolling foothills of Pennsylvania to the wilds of North Dakota, they were able to talk by phone as much as they wanted and tomorrow, Evie would get on a plane and travel to visit them, to meet her new daughter-in-law for the first time in person. She couldn't wait.

*

Pennsylvania

The flight to Philadelphia's busy airport was uneventful, though the Evie's wolf half didn't like being cramped up in a metal tube with so many strange smells. Still, the reward of seeing her son again would be worth it all in the end.

Joshua was there, waiting for her when she came off the plane. She hugged him hard, stifling the tears that wanted to flow at seeing her precious boy again. Even though he was well over six feet tall and mated now, to her, he would always be her little boy.

"You look happy," she told him when she finally stepped back, out of his embrace.

He smiled as if sharing a secret. "That's because I am happy."

The truth ringing in his worlds made her heart fill with joy. She wanted only the best for her son, including a true mate that brought this kind of sparkle to his eyes.

"Well, where is she?" Evie teased.

"Deena sends her apologies for not making the trip, but she couldn't leave the animals on their own. The little calf she took in had a problem last night and she's been sitting with him all morning, coaxing him back from the brink. If she'd left, he probably would have died and I have to admit, I'm kind of attached to the little fella now."

"A calf?" Evie had to laugh as Joshua took her rolling bag and started walking toward the exit.

"You'll understand when you get to the farm. It's the oddest conglomeration of critters you ever saw, but somehow they've formed a little barn house family." He was shaking his head now, even as he smiled.

"And they aren't afraid of you?" She didn't have to say why. One didn't talk about being a werewolf out in public where any passerby might hear.

"Not anymore. I'm not sure why they've accepted me, but they have. I almost feel like the trusty old sheepdog sometimes, but I don't mind. It would've been hard on Deena if I didn't get along with her animal family."

Evie loved the way Joshua talked about his mate. His words demonstrated the kind of consideration Evie expected of a true mating and it was good to hear.

"Then there's all the wedding prep going on. Deena's been doing it all on her own, but I think things will kick into high gear when her family starts arriving in a few days."

"Haven't you been helping?" Evie asked her son, frowning. "I never had a big wedding, but I know such things can't be done all on one's own. I would think the least you could do was help your mate set things up."

Josh put his arm around her shoulders and squeezed her to his side. Her son was so tall and broad of shoulder. As big as his father now that he was grown. He made her feel petite, though at five-foot-nine, she wasn't at all short by human standards.

"Don't worry, Mom. I'm helping. I've already done more furniture moving, laundry hauling and floor mopping than I care to admit. Deena is putting everybody up on the farm and she wanted the house cleaned top to bottom before you got here. We also had to clear out some junk that had piled up in the guest rooms and other parts of the house where we can stash guests. I even enlisted some help from the Amish neighbors to help me build a few more wooden bed frames."

Evie smiled at the idea of her big, strapping son working alongside a bunch of Amish men. She didn't doubt that Josh could accomplish anything he set his mind to, but he'd never really been big into carpentry. Oh, he'd done the odd repair job around the house, but he hadn't ever built furniture from scratch.

"Sounds like you've been busy," she said with approval of his industriousness. She knew her son would be a good mate, but the way he'd sounded before, she'd been concerned. Deena sounded lovely on the phone, but Evie intended to be a good mother-in-law and make sure Deena got what she needed from her shifter mate.

Deena was a priestess. Human. And part fey, apparently. That's why their magic had meshed so well. When Josh had finally discovered his fey side—the magic inheritance from his father—he'd sought help, and that had set him on the path that had eventually led him to Deena.

Evie was glad. She hadn't told Josh much about his father because it hurt to talk about Ray. He'd disappeared before Josh was even born and he'd taken half of Evie's heart with him...wherever he'd gone.

Maybe it hadn't been right to never discuss Ray with Josh, but it had never really been an issue until the wild magic appeared. Josh was fully grown when that had happened, and far from home. Even if Evie had been there, she wouldn't have readily recognized the cause of Josh's sudden problem. She'd always just assumed that if fey traits had been going to show up in Josh, they would have from the very beginning.

Apparently, she'd been wrong about that. She felt terrible about it now, of course, but Josh had forgiven her and it had all worked out. Josh and Deena both tried to tell Evie that they thought it had all been part of some divine plan, but Evie still wasn't sure. She felt guilty and embarrassed that her heartbreak had prevented her from even speaking Ray's name to his son for so long.

She intended to fix all that now, on this extended vacation with her son and his new mate. She had brought the few things of

Ray's that she still had. She would give them to Josh now, and tell him as much as she could remember about his father. They'd have time...and it was *about* time, too.

"Did you bring luggage?" Josh asked as they rode an escalator down to a lower level.

"Well, I had to put the presents somewhere," she replied, grinning at him.

To read more, get your copy of **Snow Magic** *by Bianca D'Arc.*

ABOUT THE AUTHOR

Bianca D'Arc has run a laboratory, climbed the corporate ladder in the shark-infested streets of lower Manhattan, studied and taught martial arts, and earned the right to put a whole bunch of letters after her name, but she's always enjoyed writing more than any of her other pursuits. She grew up and still lives on Long Island, where she keeps busy with an extensive garden, several aquariums full of very demanding fish, and writing her favorite genres of paranormal, fantasy and sci-fi romance.

Bianca loves to hear from readers and can be reached through Twitter (@BiancaDArc), Facebook (BiancaDArcAuthor) or through the various links on her website.

WELCOME TO THE D'ARC SIDE...
WWW.BIANCADARC.COM

OTHER BOOKS
BY BIANCA D'ARC

Paranormal Romance

Brotherhood of Blood
One & Only
Rare Vintage
Phantom Desires
Sweeter Than Wine
Forever Valentine
Wolf Hills*
Wolf Quest

Tales of the Were
Lords of the Were
Inferno
Lone Wolf
Snow Magic

Tales of the Were ~ The Others
Rocky
Slade
The Jaguar Tycoon

Tales of the Were ~ Redstone Clan
The Purrfect Stranger
Grif
Red
Magnus
Bobcat
Matt

Tales of the Were ~ String of Fate
Cat's Cradle
King's Throne
Jacob's Ladder
Her Warriors

Tales of the Were ~ Grizzly Cove
All About the Bear
Mating Dance
Night Shift
Alpha Bear
Saving Grace
Bearliest Catch
The Bear's Healing Touch
The Luck of the Shifters
Badass Bear

Gifts of the Ancients: Warrior's Heart

Guardians of the Dark
Half Past Dead
Once Bitten, Twice Dead
A Darker Shade of Dead
The Beast Within
Dead Alert

Epic Fantasy Erotic Romance

Dragon Knights
Maiden Flight*
The Dragon Healer
Border Lair
Master at Arms
The Ice Dragon**
Prince of Spies***
Wings of Change
FireDrake
Dragon Storm
Keeper of the Flame
Hidden Dragons

Futuristic Erotic Romance

Resonance Mates
Hara's Legacy**
Davin's Quest
Jaci's Experiment
Grady's Awakening
Harry's Sacrifice

* RT Book Reviews Awards Nominee
** EPPIE Award Winner
*** CAPA Award Winner

WWW.BIANCADARC.COM